MW00763667

CHRISTMAS KEEPERS

CORONA PUBLISHING COMPANY

Christmas Keepers

Eight Memorable Stories
from
The 40's and 50's

by

MARGARET COUSINS

CONTENTS

FOREWORD

Of all the writers who penned the fiction that filled this country's women's magazines fifty years ago, few were more prolific than Margaret Cousins. And none more warmly received by readers or more affectionately remembered by colleagues, I among them.

Maggie arrived in New York City fresh from her native Texas early in her career and never turned her back on those values and perceived virtues when she wrote of a small-town America.

But in daily life, she gave her heart to New York City, determined to gentle that giant city to a crawl. And the medium Maggie used to win the city was the same she used to win her readers: Love.

But now the author's stories face fifty years of radical lifestyle change, social shifts, and spreading sophistication—do these suggest perhaps a bridge too far? The answer lies in this small volume. Maggie Cousins reaches out and touches us once again, through the narrow window of wonder called Christmas. We must set aside our prideful worldliness. Let Maggie take us by the hand and read to us her evergreen holiday tales, where lost souls find themselves and wise young women guide their foolish fumbling men to happy ever-afters.

Santa lives.

JOHN MACK CARTER
formerly Editor-in-Chief of *Good Housekeeping*

vii

CHRISTMAS KEEPERS

The Homemade Miracle

The little town of Chester made an agreeable sight under its light, crystalline fall of snow. Every house wore a ruff of icicles and all the dark blue spruces were bearded with the damp ermine of the season. Doorways burgeoned with wreaths of green, glossy holly, and through the lamplit windows you could see Christmas trees being set up in cheerful living rooms, with families gathered before crackling fires and round-eyed children unwrapping spun-glass balls, brought down in a box from the attic, and squabbling over tinsel stars. In the high school auditorium the Choral Club was practicing its repertoire of carols and the thin, sweet sound of "Oh, Little Town of Bethlehem" drifted across the snow. In the firehouse, Chester's two blue-shirted firemen were patiently mending desiccated toys for the deserving poor. In front of the impressive stone mansion with the high wall around it on the edge of town, a weary electrician was wiring a tall guardian fir with strings of red and green lights. The illuminated display window of Dellinger's Drugstore, crowded with festive merchandise and centered by a small, elegant alligator toilet case fitted out with plastic implements of beauty, made long, glancing lights across the icy sidewalk. Above the piercing steeple of old St. John's Church brooded the blue-white radiance of the Christmas star. It was three nights before Christmas, and if you could have written Peace on Earth, Good Will to Men at the bottom of Chester, you would have had a first-rate Christmas card.

But you couldn't write it. Nobody knew that better than the Reverend Dr. Ernest Jellicoe, clergy of Chester, who was at that moment sitting on the floor in the cold, unlighted church, massaging his shinbone. For the fourth time, Dr. Jellicoe had caught his toe in the worn and threadbare carpet in front of the pulpit and fallen sprawling. He had been en route to the manse after a meeting with the Committee on the Community Christmas Tree, a tradition in Chester for more than a hundred years, and he had taken a short cut through the church auditorium to save unnecessary portage on his heavy heart.

The perquisites of his calling denied Dr.

Jellicoe the relief of profanity, but he was in the mood. He was a short-legged, jolly little man, with a rusty thatch of hair, bright blue eyes, and a disposition of belligerent cheerfulness. But now, as he sat nursing his damaged member, the memory of the bickerings, backbiting, and quarrelsomeness of the committee charged with the celebration of the Lord's Birthday in Chester still ringing in his ears, it seemed to him that St. John's Church was literally falling to pieces. Indeed, the carpet had long since fallen to pieces, and Dr. Jellicoe had now fallen among them.

He stopped deprecating the obtuse pettiness of Mrs. Brittain, Mrs. McManus, Mr. Philbert, and Mr. Dellinger long enough to wonder why the spirit didn't move the hard hearts of some of his wealthy parishioners, Mr. and Mrs. Turner, or the McManuses, or the Philberts, to give the church a new carpet. Or Miss Leonora Webb, for instance. Her great-great-grandfather had founded the church, and Dr. Jellicoe, in a rush of peevishness probably induced by his smarting tibia, considered that Miss Leonora spent enough on that illtempered Persian cat of hers to keep this humble temple in unaccustomed luxury. As he mused thus, he sighed. Miss Leonora hadn't been in the church for five years. She had vowed never to set foot in it again.

Dr. Jellicoe chewed on these morose thoughts until it occurred to him that he was a sinful and undeserving minister to be concerned with anything so worldly as a raddled carpet, when the spiritual side of his community was in the shape it was in. A sense of his own failure swept over Dr. Jellicoe, and in a rush of remorseful feeling he clambered from a sitting position to his knees and prayed for guidance in knitting together the unhappy factions and sub-factions of his parish. He prayed for a new birth of truth, justice, and good will, the wiping out of misunderstandings and misery, the demolition of snobbery and self-ishness, the revival of love and goodness.

"But it would take a miracle," Dr. Jellicoe opined in an afterthought which he did not address directly to the ears of the Almighty. "It would take a miracle."

As he got up and felt his way out of the dark church, he thought how wonderful it would be if everybody in St. John's was like Miss Smollett, the organist . . . sweet, tireless Miss Smollett with her wide, innocent gray eyes and her small, patient hands, which were never still. As he turned in at the manse, Dr. Jellicoe felt forlorn and lonely. It seemed to him that nobody in the world cared a whit for him. Christmas was always hard since Eva died.

Young Mrs. Brittain's problems were some-what different from Dr. Jellicoe's, but she had her problems. As soon as the committee meeting had subsided, Mrs. Brittain had sprinted out of the church and made tracks with her galoshes across the snow. She was so tired she could drop and she had so much to do. Mrs. Brittain had only been married a year, and all Tom's folks were coming for Christmas dinner.

She was now posed in front of a card table, all but obscured by billows of tissue paper, swirls of red and green ribbon, boxes of neckties, handkerchiefs, men's shirts, dusting powder, sachet bags, silk lingerie, books, and children's games, and she was feverishly wrapping packages while she reported to Mr. Brittain the goings on at the meeting. Tom Brittain was lolled comfortably back in an armchair, trying to read a newspaper. A box of seals had vibrated off the table, and the rug was spattered with silver stars. Mrs. Brittain was constantly scratching around among the debris because whatever she wanted—scissors, fountain pen, liquid cement—seemed to be lost.

As she delicately licked at the repulsive, mucilaginous back of the forty-fifth Christmas sticker, she eyed Tom resentfully and wondered why she had ever married a man who had two brothers, two sisters, and countless nephews and nieces, all of whom had to be remembered, and also why Mr. Brittain would not take a more active part in Chester's civic affairs. A lawyer ought to. Now, he wasn't even listening.

"We almost came to blows," young Mrs. Brittain said proudly, "but we won. After all, there have been real candles on the Chester Community Christmas Tree for a hundred years. It's just part of Christmas. It wouldn't be the same with electric lights. You know it wouldn't, Thomas. It would just destroy the whole spirit of the occasion. Don't you think so?"

"Huh?" Mr. Brittain said, out of the depths of his newspaper.

Mrs. Brittain sighed and went over the whole thing again, adding fervor to her recital.

"Not very safe, if you ask me," Mr. Brittain announced.

"What?" Mrs. Brittain interrogated coldly.

"Candles," said Mr. Brittain.

Mrs. Brittain compressed her nice red mouth into a thin line. That was the trouble with Tom— always on the practical side. She was a romantic little thing herself. But Tom just refused to appreciate the finer sensibilities—like wrapping presents. Tom said it was just a waste of time. People tore into them without even looking at the frills and furbelows.

"Hold your finger on this knot," Mrs. Brittain ordered grimly. "I have to tie a bow."

She might have expected Mrs. McManus and Mr. Philbert to be against her. But Tom!

Mr. Brittain threw down his paper with an angry rustle, got up and lumbered over to the card table with obvious reluctance. He stuck his finger down on the box which Mrs. Brittain was holding with such force that one leg of the card table wobbled and collapsed and the manifold items on it, including the jar of rubber cement, cascaded to the floor.

"Oh, Tom!" Mrs. Brittain cried in dismay. "How could you be so clumsy?"

She could have wept with exasperation at the mess, and Mr. Brittain, now furious to have his quiet evening at home despoiled, stalked out of the room and pounded up the stairs without a backward look.

Mrs. Brittain got down on the floor on all fours and groveled among the scattered packages, seals, tags, tissue paper, ribbon, and rubber cement, intent on salvage. The cement had attached itself to practically every item in the pile and was now seeping merrily into the rug. Everything she touched stuck to her, and Mrs. Brittain finally sat down on the floor and succumbed to tears of weariness and rage. She thought about the beautiful flannel smoking jacket she had skimped and saved from the household budget to buy for Tom. It was as soft and warm as fleece. She had loved it. Now she almost wished she had her money back.

"I bet he hasn't got a thing for me," she sniffled in self-pity. He was notoriously thoughtless. "Oh, Tom, our first Christmas too!"

As a matter of fact, he didn't. Poor thing. Uncomfortably ensconced in a slipper chair in the bedroom, trying to read the paper by a frivolous boudoir lamp, Mr. Brittain found he could not keep his mind on the news. He was too preoccupied with wondering what was the matter with

Patty to make her so cross and irritable lately and what in the world he could give her for Christmas. Mr. Brittain went over in his mind a long list of possible presents for Patty and discarded each one as not good enough. He was in a terrible funk.

Mrs. Brittain cried quietly for a few minutes and then she lifted her head and sniffed, scrambled to her feet, and tore out to the kitchen. Her fruit cake was burning.

Five minutes later she came back with a scrubbing bucket to get at the rubber cement. The light of battle glowed in her tear-stained hazel eyes. The fruit cake was definitely burned and it was all Tom's fault.

"He's mean," Mrs. Brittain muttered. "I don't know why I never noticed it before."

One more feud had been added to Chester's overwhelming category.

"Stand still," Mrs. McManus complained to Evelyn, her squirming seven-year-old, through a mouthful of pins. "If your costume hikes up in front, you won't look much like an angel!"

Mrs. McManus was gathering folds of white cheesecloth around Evelyn's tubby middle and sewing loops on the shoulders in order to affix a pair of gilded wings lying beside her on the sofa.

"I'm tired," Evelyn whined.

"*You're* tired," Mrs. McManus said bitterly. "All you have to do is stand here while I fit this. I have to finish these two costumes tonight. The dress rehearsal for the pageant is tomorrow. There, I guess that will do."

She lifted the dress over Evelyn's head. "I can't think," Mrs. McManus said to Mr. McManus, "what Miss Smollett means having that Cermak child in the Angels' Chorus. I don't know what this town is coming to."

"What's the matter with the Cermak child?" Mr. McManus inquired mildly. "Is she catching?"

"Curtis, you know very well the Cermaks are Polish immigrants. Foreigners!"

"Anna was born right here in Chester," Mr. McManus reminded her. "I remember it well. Her mother died."

Mrs. McManus brushed this off. "I'm sure she hasn't got a pair of white shoes to her name. It will ruin the looks of the chorus. And she stands right next to Evelyn too."

"All God's chillun haven't got white shoes," Mr. McManus paraphrased wittily.

"Curtis, you're simply impossible," Mrs. McManus retorted, more huffed than ever to seem in the wrong. "As a mother, I simply must think of the future of my children. . . ."

"What has the future got to do with day after tomorrow?" Curtis McManus asked with some heat. "Joe Cermak is a good man. There's not a better man or a better worker in town. He's done a fine job bringing up that brood of orphan kids. You women make me sick!"

Mrs. McManus stopped speaking to her husband.

"Come here, Freddy," she ordered peremptorily.

Freddy McManus was rolling on the floor with Whiskers, his spotted fox terrier, shaking the house with the fervor of their rough-and-tumble.

"Aw, what for?" Freddy asked plaintively. "What for, Mother?"

Whiskers cocked his head, barked, and lunged at Freddy. More floor rolling, yells, and staccato barks.

"I want to fit your costume," Mrs. McManus shouted over the melee.

"Aw, Mother," Freddy complained for the twentieth time. "I don't want to be an angel."

"Bow wow wow wow yap!" Whiskers barked fiercely and seized the tail of Freddy's cheese-cloth robe.

"I don't think there is any real danger," Curtis inserted.

"You're an archangel," Mrs. McManus informed her recalcitrant son severely. "Wait a minute. I've got to think of some way to make this halo stay on."

"I'm afraid that's hopeless, Vera," Curtis said.

"Curtis, will you please hush," Mrs. McManus cried irritably. "You're just making the whole thing more difficult."

"What's an archangel?" Evelyn asked. "What's an archangel, Mother?"

"Well—it's—er—kind of a special angel. Be still, Fred."

"What are archangels, Daddy?" Evelyn

repeated, dissatisfied.

"Archangels are the angels' head men, Evie," Curtis said. "Angel captains of angel teams."

"Curtis, there is no necessity for being sacrilegious." Mrs. McManus was working desperately with a wire which elevated the gilded paper halo over Frederick's ruffled mop.

"If I hafta wear an old costume, why can't I be Flash Gordon?" Freddy asked. "He goes up in the sky in a rocket."

Mrs. McManus looked distraught, even a little terrified. "This is a serious pageant, Freddy," she rebuked him. "You have learned about angels in Sunday school. I don't want you to make remarks like that about such things."

"Maybe Miss Smollett would let him be Lucifer," Curtis put in. "He seems to be absolutely suited for that role."

"Lucifer! I'm Lucifer," Freddy cried, dancing around in his halo. Whiskers cocked his ears at this new game and broke into loud barks. The halo slid forward and settled over Freddy's forehead at a cockeyed angle.

"Stop that racket!" Mrs. McManus shouted, undone at last. "You're giving me a terrible headache. Curtis, you simply encourage them."

Freddy pranced round and round the room, joined by Evelyn and followed by Whiskers, jumping and barking. In the middle of the scene of carnage, the doorbell burst into a loud peal.

Curtis opened the door and was greeted by the

sight of the entire Chester constabulary, a man named Ed Moore.

"Is that your dog?" Mr. Moore inquired.

Whiskers walked over and smelled his boots delicately. Freddy stood frozen to the spot, his face pale, his halo tipped ludicrously over one eye.

"It is," Curtis answered. "Why?"

"Is that your boy?"

"Yes," Curtis admitted.

"Got a complaint from Miss Leonora Webb about him," Mr. Moore stated lugubriously. "Claims your boy set your dog on her cat."

Freddy picked up Whiskers and clutched him convulsively against his chest. Evie stared round-eyed at the policeman. Mrs. McManus let out a low moan. "Miss Leonora Webb!"

"Yup," said Mr. Moore. "Sets great store by that cat of hers."

"Did you do that, Fred?" his father asked.

"Well—uh," Freddy dissembled. "Dad, you know how Whiskers is about cats. I didn't set him on it—exactly. I mean he just kind of ran after Miss Webb's old cat. In a way."

"Fred, you know what I think about cruelty," Curtis told him. "Go to your room. I'll attend to you later."

Freddy started out, still holding Whiskers in a death grip.

"Leave the dog here," Curtis said.

"Aw, Dad, let me take him."

"No."

Freddy's eyes filled with tears. "Dad," he pleaded, "you aren't going to do anything to Whiskers. Dad, you won't let him take Whiskers away." Freddy's face corrugated with the horror of this thought.

"I'll take care of Whiskers."

"Just keep him penned up," Mr. Moore said kindly. "Just came by to give you a warning. You know how Miss Leonora Webb is—always mixed up in city politics. Got to pay attention to her. Now me, I don't see a thing wrong with it. Most natural thing in the world. Sets too much store by that darned old cat, anyway."

Dragging up the stairs, Freddy felt relieved, but he looked forward with no anticipation to the impending session, and his hopes for a Christmas bicycle went glimmering.

For years nothing had gone right for Miss Leonora Webb. Sometimes she thought that everything happened to her, but if she had analyzed it more closely, she might have come to the conclusion that not enough happened. As a matter of fact, Miss Leonora was a typical old maid, though nobody in Chester would have dared admit it, least of all Leonora herself. She was still the little princess of the Webb castle, surrounded by its high stone walls with their lodge gates of grilled iron. Miss Leonora was forty-five now and reigned alone. Her father and mother and brother were dead, and a suitor capable of subduing

Miss Leonora's proud heart had never presented himself.

Miss Leonora was the rock upon which the social wave of Chester split.

She was a handsome woman who wore smart clothes purchased on semi-annual trips to Chicago, and up to five years ago she had taken a large part in all of Chester's affairs. At that time she had had a falling out with Mrs. Wilford Turner, her best friend and president of the St. John's Ladies League, over the decorations of the church for Easter Sunday.

The quarrel had started over some minor issue and had progressed to dimensions possible only in a town the size of Chester. The fact that Ada Turner was the nearest thing to a sister Leonora had ever had merely made matters worse. Eventually they had stopped speaking and Miss Leonora had refused to set foot in St. John's Church ever since.

Now every party in Chester was complicated by the fact that Ada Turner and Leonora Webb wouldn't be caught dead in the same room with each other. It was a hurdle that each harried hostess had to clear, but they accepted it with resignation. It was just part of Chester tradition. Both Ada and Leonora had their followers, and all public questions in Chester saw them line up like two sides of a spelling bee and form a deadlock.

But in St. John's, Ada Turner ruled the roost. Miss Leonora just stayed away.

Miss Webb lived in the big stone house on the outskirts of Chester with her niece, Kathleen, aged nineteen and submissive, and her cat, a rambunctious feline appropriately named Jezebel. Kathleen was a sweet, pretty girl with eyes like damp violets and she had afforded Miss Leonora much pleasure until lately, when she seemed to have become overnight silent, moody, and withdrawn. Sometimes she came down to breakfast looking as if she had been crying. Miss Leonora, who never bothered to understand other people— she understood herself perfectly—had no way of supposing that Kathleen was in the throes of love and anguish. Miss Leonora would certainly not have supposed that the cause of the trouble was one Wilford Turner, Jr., with whom Kathleen had made the inevitable and perfectly natural error of falling in love.

Miss Leonora lived in a perpetual outrage, but today was the last straw. It wasn't enough that Jezebel had come home bedraggled and bleeding from a dogfight, obviously set in motion by that execrable McManus boy, but now Kathleen wanted to go to that ridiculous Community Christmas Tree at St. John's.

Miss Leonora was so mad she could have spit, if it had been a ladylike thing to do, but instead, she sat and fumed and tried to elicit from Kathleen the reason why, after all she had done for her, she would wish to go against her devoted aunt's wishes.

It was impossible for Kathleen to explain that she hadn't seen Willie Turner for three weeks, after they, like everyone else, had split on the rock of Miss Leonora, and that she felt fairly certain of at least getting a look at him at St. John's and letting him get a look at her. The name of Turner was the word taboo in the Webb household. So Kathleen sat silent, sticking her chin out slightly and showing, for the first time, the Webb stubborn streak.

Kathleen was already sorry that she had refused to elope with Wilford Turner, Jr., on December first, risking the loss of his patrimony and certainly cutting herself off forever from Miss Leonora, whom she had the misfortune to love dearly. (She certainly wasn't the old dragon Willie had called her.) Now it was too late, Kathleen thought, sobbing inwardly. The Chester grapevine had already brought it to her attention that Willie was beauing the Masons' visitor—a sleek post-debutante from Chicago named Marcia Garrison. Kathleen reflected with frenzy that Miss Garrison was probably only amusing herself with Wilford Turner, since she was beautiful and must have a dozen men at home, but she told herself that she could not bear the idea of anybody trifling with Wilford's gentle heart. Besides, he was so wonderful, who was Marcia Garrison to resist him?

Kathleen was sick with misery and stunned with love and would willingly have thrown over

Miss Leonora and her comfortable home to start anywhere with Willie. But what could she do? He didn't call. He didn't come. And she had waited until she could bear it no longer.

Miss Leonora was brushing out Jezebel's matted fur with a brush, and Kathleen was being stubborn.

"I guess that will teach you to let dogs alone," Miss Leonora said firmly to Jezebel, and Kathleen started, feeling somehow that the epithet had been applied to her precious Willie. Her lip quivered.

"I declare, Kathleen," Miss Leonora said, "I don't know what's got into you, moping and sniffling around the house, and now this business of the Christmas tree. I can't think why you want to go to that again."

"I've been going all my life," Kathleen said defensively. "Ever since I was a little girl."

"You certainly haven't been lately," Miss Leonora pointed out. "Besides, you're a big girl now."

Kathleen got up out of the Victorian armchair and stood there, looking every inch a Webb. She stuck her chin out a little further—although the fact that it was quivering like the nose of a rabbit hardly added to the desired effect of granite determination—and said, "Well, I'm going. So there. You can't stop me!" Whereupon she rushed out of the room.

Miss Leonora shook her head in pure astonishment. Jezebel twitched, arched her back, and jumped noiselessly from Miss Leonora's lap to the padded carpet. Jezebel also left the room, waving her tail with arrogance.

"I'll never in the world understand either women or cats," Miss Leonora announced to the empty spaces. She got up militantly, marched into the baronial dining room, and sat down at one end of the long table to her solitary dinner. For a brief, distracted instant Miss Leonora felt like a lonely, cast-off old woman. She jerked herself erect and trod on the bell with unnecessary vigor, but the notion persisted.

"What is the matter with everybody?" Miss Leonora asked herself with rising anger.

Mr. Dellinger was standing behind the counter of his drugstore worrying about business. Mr. Dellinger was a natural-born worrier about business. It was one of his principal activities, although his business went along fine from year to year. He wasn't setting the world afire, but he made a good living for Mrs. Dellinger and the boys. He was progressive, too, and tried out a lot of the new things he read in the trade magazines. He was what you might call a prominent citizen—whenever Chester did anything he was always in the big middle of it. But there was that too. People didn't seem to be paying him as much attention as they used to. They asked his advice and then they didn't take it. He worried about this for a while, but pretty soon he got back to business. It had more angles.

The thing that was worrying him especially right now was the alligator cosmetic kit which which was the pièce de résistance of his holiday line. It was marked $49.50, and it now seemed to Mr. Dellinger that nobody in Chester was going to pay nearly fifty dollars for a Christmas present for anybody. He had simply let that salesman overpersuade him. Mr. Dellinger peered sadly over the shoulder of the cardboard Santa Claus into the window and regarded the beautiful brown case with its fabulous appointments. Mr. Dellinger wished ardently that it was back in the sample room of the wholesale drug house where it had come from.

While he brooded he noticed a couple walking along the deserted street, probably just out of the last show at the Chester Palace Theatre. When they came abreast of the window they stopped and looked in. He observed that the girl was tall and sophisticated-looking and had on a startling hat made out of some kind of dark fur, in which a jeweled ornament blazed. Her red mouth curved into a smile as she gesticulated toward the window, and he saw with a thrill of anticipation that her brown eyes were going over the alligator kit. It was that Chicago girl who was visiting Mrs. Mason—name of Garrison or some such. The man with her was Willie Turner.

They were laughing and Willie was holding the

fur-clad arm of the tall, striking girl. Mr. Dellinger didn't know whether he liked that or not. Everybody in town except Mrs. Turner and Miss Leonora Webb knew that Kathleen Webb and Willie Turner were supposed to be in love with each other. Mr. Dellinger's loyalty to Chester rose in his throat, and he deprecated the idea of some city woman coming to Chester and poaching on the preserves of a hometown girl. Especially Kathleen.

As the couple sauntered on, Mr. Dellinger added this item to his worry about business, worrying first one and then the other.

About fifteen minutes before midnight, just as he was fixing up to close for the night, a solitary figure came through the doorway and stepped up to the counter. It was Willie Turner.

"Hello, Mr. Dellinger," Willie greeted. "I wonder if I could see that brown alligator case in the window."

Mr. Dellinger was host to a complicated emotion. It looked as if he was actually going to get rid of that kit, but plagued if he wanted to sell it to Willie Turner to give to that stiff-necked Miss Garrison. Why, it would break Kathleen's heart! Everybody in town knew about that kit. It had been in the window for two weeks with the price plainly marked on it—$49.50. It was the most expensive present in Chester, and there had been considerable speculation about the lucky recipient. If Miss Garrison carried it off, it would certainly be a blow to Chester womanhood.

Mr. Dellinger ambled over to the window and removed the kit from its nest of red satin and set it on the counter.

Willie picked up the handsome plastic hair-brush.

"It's pretty," Willie said, running his hand over the leather. "Is it real alligator?"

Mr. Dellinger was staggered by his own answer. "Can't say," he replied. "Not sure of it."

Was that the way to be a super-salesman? What would that trade-journal editor think of him, quashing his own sale? Of course it was alligator, but Mr. Dellinger suddenly could not bear the idea of having the kit fall into Miss Garrison's hands.

"How much?" Willie asked, purely as a matter of routine.

"It's $49.50," Mr. Dellinger said. "Too much, if you ask me."

"I'll take it," Willie decided and Mr. Dellinger felt as if he had received an uppercut to the jaw.

"No exchanges or refunds," he reminded Willie grimly, hoping he might change his mind.

"I'll take it along with me." Willie ignored the interruption, laid five tens on the counter.

Mr. Dellinger wrapped up the case and put the money in the cash register, gave Willie fifty cents, and watched him go off with his purchase. Before him swam Kathleen's small, sensitive face. He felt like a traitor. He felt worse. There was a time

when he could mold public opinion. He had tried
to keep from selling Willie the kit, although it
would have represented a personal loss to him,
but Willie had simply brushed him off. He didn't
mean anything in this town any more. He had out-
lived his usefulness.

"I'm slipping," Mr. Dellinger thought wildly as
he locked the front door. "I must be slipping."

Miss Dora Smollett felt as if every bone in her
body would break. She was so tired, and the
pageant had been such a mess tonight. How in the
world could she ever whip it in shape by
Christmas Eve? Miss Smollett dragged back her
nice curly hair and began to slap cold cream on
her face. As she did so, she minutely examined
the lines in her forehead and sighed audibly. She
was just thirty-six, but already the wrinkles were
getting embedded.

Miss Smollett looked around her chaste bedroom and wondered if her life were going to be
like this always—teaching school five days a
week and playing the organ on Sunday and every
minute in between getting up programs and enter-
tainments for Chester consumption. Not that she
didn't love her work, and Dr. Jellicoe was so
appreciative of her efforts. He was a darling,
really, and lonely since he lost his wife three years
ago.

She thought happily about Dr. Jellicoe for a
few minutes—how he always backed her up.

Tonight, for instance, when that stuck-up Mrs. McManus didn't want Anna Cermak in the Angels' Chorus, Dr. Jellicoe had been behind her one hundred per cent, in spite of the fact that Mrs. McManus was on the school board and a power in the church. Anna Cermak had the best voice in Chester, but Dr. Jellicoe didn't know that. He had just backed up Miss Smollett. Oh, he was such a good man, but so shy.

Miss Smollett had gotten to the place where she actually dreaded Christmas. Christmas seemed to consist entirely of carols and pageants, with the children acting like limbs of Satan and their parents not acting much better. If she had a child . . .

Miss Smollett stopped short. It was a strange thing that Miss Smollett, whose waking hours were full of children, mostly brats, too, still wanted a child more than anything. A home, a husband, and a child. That was all life amounted to. A husband like Dr. Jellicoe—gentle and kind and affectionate. He loved children, and he had never had any. His first wife had been delicate.

She thought of a little boy with Dr. Jellicoe's rusty red hair and belligerent blue eyes and sighed. She put her elbows on the window sill and looked out across the snow to the white spire of St. John's with the low-lying bulk of the manse hard by. There was a subdued yellow light burning in the back window of the manse. She yearned toward it.

In a moment she blushed deeply, jumped up, and snapped off the light and got in bed, shivering. She pulled the blankets up to her throat and buried her face in the pillow.

The little town of Chester lay silent and lightless under the tremendous navy-blue arc of the winter sky. A few snowflakes fluttered desultorily to earth, piled a little higher on the loaded arms of the blue spruces. In a hundred quiet houses the mysterious processes of life went on—the light, shallow breathing of the sleepers, a child's arm flung out over the coverlet, a man's head settling into the curve of a woman's arm, restless, unconscious turning in a narrow bed, tears dampening a pillow, eyes staring into the dark while a mind turned a problem over and over, a lonely cough, dreams.

Whiskers woke briefly from a vision of celestial cat-chasing, yawned, and stretched himself stiffly in front of the dying embers in the McManus fireplace. Jezebel, prowling the wide rooms of the Webb mansion, her green eyes glowing in the sentient dark, felt her fur rise suddenly on her back, as if in premonition of some momentous event. Jezebel paused and looked behind her, troubled with memories of the afternoon. Then, her sharp nails clicking on the parquet floors, she sought her basket in the butler's pantry, jumped in, and, curling herself into a ball, she slept.

All over Chester there was a period of supreme hush.

The day before Christmas Eve dawned with flurries of snow and everything else. Harried housewives checked and rechecked lists— Christmas-present lists, grocery lists, invitation lists, lists of things to do today. Men sat down to sketchy hurried meals, looking morose at the abandonment of life's safe and regular routine. Children were bundled off to school, threatened with dire consequences if they took off their galoshes. The name of Santa Claus was taken many times in vain.

Kitchens exuded the smell of spice and rising cakes, and many a fatted turkey met its predestined fate. Cranberries burbled on the backs of stoves, and the sound of the eggbeater was rife in Chester. Shopping in Chester's half dozen stores was at fever pitch. Sales people thought their feet would simply come off while dilatory ladies made up their minds. The populace was very cross.

In the warehouse on Center Street, a committee from the Merchants' Luncheon Club, to which every adult male in town belonged whether he was a merchant or not, was packing baskets for Chester's needy.

"Lots of beans, men," Mr. Philbert, the vice-president of the First National Bank, advised. "That'll stick to their ribs."

"Put in some oranges," young Dr. Redding urged. "They need vitamins—those kids."

They looked at Dr. Redding rather coldly. He was new in town. Came about six months ago to take over old Doc Patterson's practice, but he looked so young nobody who could afford to pay a doctor sent for him. They got Dr. Pierson to come over from Mason, twelve miles away. A kid like Dr. Redding couldn't know much.

"Oranges—mighty high," Gordy Stevens of Stevens Brothers Grocery demurred. "Forty-five cents a dozen."

"They ought to have oranges," Dr. Redding insisted stubbornly. "I—I'll buy two dozen. One orange for each basket."

Everybody knew he couldn't afford it. He was just putting up a front. They didn't think much of that. Kind of upstart.

"I'll buy a crate of oranges for the baskets," Curtis McManus said. "Put me down for a crate."

They switched their disapproval from Dr. Redding to Curtis.

"Don't know if we'll have enough," Gordy Stevens said. "Got to save two crates for the Community Christmas Tree."

"Why?" Curtis demanded wrathfully. "Every kid at the Community Christmas Tree gets his vitamins."

"It's the custom," Gordy said. "Everybody at the Community Christmas Tree gets an orange and an apple. Been doing it for a hundred years, I guess."

"Maybe it's time we changed," Curtis pursued, while Dr. Redding regarded him with the gratefulness of a puppy. "I get tired hearing about

Chester's first hundred years."

The committee looked at him aghast.

Every woman in town, with the exception of the bedridden and Miss Leonora Webb and her niece Kathleen, was buzzing around St. John's Church. At nine o'clock Joe Cermak and his oldest boy had brought the tall, splendid fir, still glistening with melted snow, to the door of the church in Joe's rattletrap truck. It was a beautiful tree, stately, majestic, and properly bushy around the bottom. It had been selected with great care and meditation by the feminine members of the Committee for the Community Christmas Tree a week before. Joe and his son, Erik, had been up by daylight to fell it with the long, swinging blows of their bright axes. Now it stood in the center of the platform, reaching high into the nave, drenched in blue light from the memorial window behind it.

Mrs. Brittain was standing on top of a stepladder, affixing dozens of red candles to its thick, bushy twigs. But Mrs. Brittain's heart was heavy. Tom had gone off to town without kissing her good-by for the first time in their married life. Christmas was spoiled—that's all—simply spoiled. She could have cried when she remembered that she had ten more hateful presents to wrap.

Mrs. Brittain reached for a high branch right in the front of the tree, and she was suddenly over-

come with an attack of nausea. She thought wildly for a minute that she was falling through space.
"Tom, Tom!" she whispered, and then the world
righted itself and she saw that she was still standing on top of the stepladder. The branch with its
red candle had already snapped back in place.

All around the tree women were busily hanging
decorations—strings of tinfoil icicles, tinsel
medallions, and artificial snow. They chattered in
high, strained voices and ran hither and yon,
wearing themselves down to a nub. Dr. Jellicoe
was there, trying to be of some use, but they all
thought privately he was just in the way and ought
to go on into his study and think up a sermon.

At noon they paused to partake of a cold lunch
in the church parlors. This was a signal for bits of
gossip, whispered behind hands, since everybody
in town worth gossiping about was there. Mrs.
Philbert thought the strings of popcorn on the tree
that Mrs. Dellinger insisted on looked tacky. Mrs.
Dellinger had heard that Gordy Stevens had been
drinking again. Mrs. Stevens said that Mrs.
Moore told her that Ed had told her Miss Leonora
Webb was on a high horse about that old cat of
hers. Mrs. Elgin wondered if Miss Leonora was
the one who had put a stop to Kathleen's seeing
that Turner boy. Mrs. West said that she heard
Willie Turner had been going with that Garrison
girl from Chicago and that was what had put a
stop to it. She looked like a wild one, all right.
Mrs. Willis had heard from a friend of hers in

Chicago that Marcia Garrison was a divorcee. Mrs. McManus still thought they should have electric lights on the Christmas tree—it would look so much smarter. That little Mrs. Brittain simply had no taste.

Dr. Jellicoe, seated at the head of the table, felt as if he were breasting a cold wind. He was lost and anxious and kept looking in every direction for a sympathetic eye to catch. Something was wrong. Something was missing. Suddenly he realized that Miss Smollett wasn't there—Miss Smollett, his ever-present help in time of trouble. Miss Smollett was teaching school today.

He passed his hand over his brow, conscious of the petty malice going its predestined rounds until it finally arrived at the place it could hurt somebody's feelings. He wondered what would happen if he stood up in his place, rapped for attention, and told them a well-worn Christmas story, that old one about good will to men. But he didn't have the courage. Tired and sad, he gulped his cooling coffee.

By three o'clock the tree was decorated and stood tall and proud in spite of the baubles which hung about it—a child of nature, bringing to the little church the sweet, spicy fragrance of the outdoors. The ladies stood back in little groups, admiring it, putting their heads on one side, and making pleased exclamations. Then they all rushed into their wraps and started home to collect the presents, which would soon be piled waist-deep round the platform.

All the adults in Chester who were within the pale exchanged their gifts at the Community Christmas Tree. It was a lot of trouble and gave rise to bitter competition as to who gave the finest presents, but they had been doing it in Chester for a hundred years. It was part of the tradition—a custom which had once been a needful social gesture but was long since outgrown. The children, who had their real Christmas along with their stockings on the following morning, received a toy or two and plenty of candy and nuts from the hands of Santa Claus himself in a red velvet suit, black fishing boots, and a spurious silver beard. Most of them knew it was Mr. Philbert, the banker, who somehow fancied himself in the role of Santa Claus and had the figure for it.

Miss Leonora watched the home-going hordes from the long casement windows in her library with a twinge of loneliness. Miss Leonora had come to despise all holidays, for at such times the whole town seemed to be against her. She missed the lovely, bossy role she had played in the past, and though she would never admit it, she missed Ada Turner, with whom she had spent many of the Christmases of her life before the falling-out. Heretofore Kathleen had contributed a note of gaiety to Miss Leonora's diminished life, but now Kathleen was as moody and morose as she was herself and was persistently keeping to her room.

Upstairs, Kathleen was wrapping and rewrapping the fine pin-seal wallet she had bought for Willie's Christmas present when she went to the city at Thanksgiving, trying to make up her mind whether or not to put it on the tree for him after all. He might think she was trying to get him back, and of course she *wasn't*. Still, what earthly use would she have for a wallet with *Wilford Turner, Jr.*, stamped on it in gold? Might as well give it to him—without a card, Kathleen decided—a last gesture to romance. When it occurred to Kathleen that Willie might think Marcia Garrison had given it to him, she winced and unwrapped it once more. Finally, she slipped it into her purse, unwrapped.

She went over to the closet to examine her clothes. She didn't have a thing to wear! What she wanted was a worldly dress, something like Marcia Garrison always wore. Kathleen examined the half dozen simple wool dresses with their little round necks and piqué collars and cuffs. How could she compete with Marcia Garrison's mink coat and jewelry in those!

"Ooooh, I'm so miserable," Kathleen moaned, and collapsed on the bed in despair.

At four o'clock Miss Smollett opened the door to the church auditorium and breathed the wonderful fragrance of the Christmas fir. Her eyes were bright, and a few fragments of her blond hair had escaped the sensible hat she wore and now lay curled against her red cheeks. Dr. Jellicoe, who had come out of his study at the sound, stood behind the Christmas tree where she couldn't see him and drank in the sight of her naïve face. His heart leaned toward hers, and then he pulled himself up short. What would everybody think—the preacher and the organist, and Eva not three years in her grave?

Miss Smollett took off her hat, laid it on the organ bench, and sat down. She pulled out several stops and began to play, and the deep-throated voice of the organ filled the room. Dr. Jellicoe closed his eyes and listened. He felt peaceful and almost happy for the first time in a long while. Then, because his mind seemed to be running entirely along secular lines, he tiptoed back into his study without speaking to her.

At four-fifteen the first aggregation of angels straggled in, sniffling from the cold and dragging their leaden galoshes. They all carried their costumes in packages and boxes, and, as soon as they had laid these down and been divested of their wraps, they became possessed of demons. They fought, scuffled, and chased each other up and down the aisles and under the pews, knocking hymnbooks and collection envelopes winding. They were trailed by their mothers, grandmothers, aunts, and sisters loaded down with Christmas presents which they began to arrange around the edge of the platform and at the foot of the tree. Thirty minutes of pandemonium mixed with discipline ensued.

In the Sunday-school room the angels were at last garbed in their robes and wings and began to look more angelic and to act even less so. The archangels kept pulling the angels' hair and dragging their cheesecloth draperies in the dust of the floor. Miss Smollett was beside herself. She dashed from the Sunday-school room to the organ and back to the basement to get old Jim Travis, the sexton, to bring up a plank and two boxes for the archangels to stand on. The angels hid them from view, and Miss Smollett knew that would never work. She had decided to put Evelyn McManus and Anna Cermak out in front. They were the smallest and their sweet, high trebles would be more effective there. They were a perfect foil for each other, Anna with her long dark hair and melting brown eyes and little Evelyn McManus, blond and pretty as a Christmas doll.

Mrs. McManus sniffed at this arrangement, in spite of the fact that Evelyn would lead the procession and had a place of utmost prominence. She looked at Anna Cermak coldly. Anna's costume was badly made, and the scuffed toes of her school shoes protruded like clodhoppers from her white draperies.

Finally the children were all lined up, and Miss Smollett struck the pitch. In the middle of "Hark! The Herald Angels Sing," Phil Stevens, Artie Philbert, and Freddy McManus got in a jostling match and knocked the plank off the boxes, whereat all the archangels fell off into the

Christmas tree. Nobody was hurt, but there were loud outcries from assembled mothers. Miss Smollett thought if her little boy acted like that she would certainly give him the flat of her hand. After this the angels got the giggles, and the dress rehearsal ended in a rout.

While the angels and archangels were dressing, their feminine relatives stacked and restacked the loot around the platform. Dr. Jellicoe, peering timorously from the study door, had a terrible tendency to think about the money-changers in the temple. But he reproached himself. They were all good people and good friends, and the offerings must be the token of Chester's good heart.

Finally everybody left except Miss Smollett, who was repairing the damages wrought by the archangels' descent into the Christmas tree. When she had finished she sat down in a pew to enjoy the Christmas tree herself for a minute. She closed her eyes and gave herself up to weariness. Time passed and she wakened with a start, realizing that she was not alone. A man was standing beside her.

It was Willie Turner.

"I'm sorry I scared you," he apologized. "I just wanted to put this on the tree, but I didn't get it wrapped up."

He held the brown alligator case toward her and looked worried.

"Oh, how beautiful," Miss Smollett said wistfully, thinking it must be wonderful to have somebody care for you fifty dollars' worth. "I'd put it on just like that. It's lovely!"

Willie was grateful. "I'm glad you like it," he said with pride. "Do you honestly think it will be all right unwrapped?"

Miss Smollett opened the case and made little cooing sounds at the sight of the beautiful pale beige lining and the handsome fittings.

"Do you know," she said, stricken with inspiration, "I'd open it like this—just the way it was in Dellinger's window. I think everybody would love to see it, just like this, close to."

She set the opened case, with the lid back, directly in the center of the mountain of presents, right at the foot of the Christmas tree.

"Do you think that's all right?" Willie asked doubtfully.

"It's just perfect," Miss Smollett declared, carried away with the idea. "It just adds the finishing touch!"

"Well, if you say so, I guess it's all right," Willie gave in. "Could I drive you home?"

"That would be awfully nice," Miss Smollett answered, and struggled into her coat.

They had a hard time getting the storm door open. It seemed to freeze in icy weather.

"I keep thinking I'll have to speak to the committee about this door," Miss Smollett said. "It's been sticking for years. And there's a window light out in the basement. I meant to tell Dr. Jellicoe."

Miss Smollett thought she ought to run by the

manse and tell Dr. Jellicoe right now, but then she thought better of it. It might seem too forward.

Christmas Eve in Chester was like Christmas Eve in any other town, except that the suppressed excitement seemed to reach even a loftier pitch, owing to the many challenges thrown down by the Community Christmas Tree. Somehow, everybody got through the day, and by eight o'clock cars were snorting up to the door of St. John's bearing the denizens of Chester and their progeny, each in his most splendid habiliments.

Mothers were too exhausted by preparations to have any hope of enjoying the occasion. Fathers were disgruntled, already anticipating the bad news in the way of statements which would roll in around January first—just when you had to pay your taxes too. Children were so wild with excitement that discipline went by the board, and their elders gave up with long, potent sighs. Young people were strangely distraught, already tasting the faint disappointment of an event built too high, knowing in their bones they weren't going to get the presents they wanted most. Quarrels were intensified, feuds more bitter, factions more pronounced. Overworked people were more overworked. Grief-stricken people found their sorrows bearing the double weight of memory. Lonely people were lonelier still.

Mr. Philbert, sweating in his red velvet suit, was in Dr. Jellicoe's study, trying to get his whiskers firmly attached. He expressed a cheer and jollity he was far from feeling. He had prudently bought his wife a government bond for Christmas and had discovered at dinner that she expected a beaver coat. A man never knows what to buy.

The angels and archangels were in the Sunday-school room, sitting gravely around the low tables under threat of a wholesale thrashing if they moved or made any noise. Every wing was in place, and the halos had not slipped appreciably. They were scrubbed and shining but ill at ease and somewhat pale around the gills at the thought of actually facing an audience. Miss Smollett, on the verge of a nervous breakdown, was coaching them in the order of the carols for the last time.

Out in front, Dr. Jellicoe was moving among his flock with apologetic hospitality, stopping to speak to every family as they sat bolt upright in their pews, staring at the Christmas tree. They were really a fine-looking group of people he told himself—genuine, honest faces, full of strong American character. But there was some kind of grim intensity about them all, as if each mind was far away, engrossed in a knotty tangle of its own. Dr. Jellicoe's gentle heart ached. He wanted to bend down and say to them all, "Don't worry. Everything will be all right."

But he wasn't sure it would.

In a back pew, a little removed, Joe Cermak was sitting with his two boys and his eldest daughter. Joe's big, simple face was lighted with pleasure at the beauty of the Christmas tree which he had cut down in the woods and for which he felt a special sort of ownership. Besides, wasn't his own Anna in the Angels' Chorus with the rest of the children? If anybody in the room was at peace with the world, it was Joe Cermak, but as Dr. Jellicoe spoke to him he was smitten with a sinking feeling. Dr. Jellicoe knew, all at once, that out of that mountain of gifts at the base of the platform there wouldn't be a one for Joe and his children. Overwrought as he was, Dr. Jellicoe would have liked to sit down and weep that such a thing could come to pass in his congregation. He was sick with regret that he hadn't anticipated such a circumstance and bought presents for them himself. Now it was too late.

"What will I do?" Dr. Jellicoe asked himself, but no answer came. He moved off down the aisle, after exchanging greetings with Joe and complimenting him on his family, in a state of desperation.

When Dr. Jellicoe stopped to speak to young Dr. Redding and his wife, Dr. Redding seemed pathetically glad. They were sitting alone, like two strangers at a feast, and nobody was saying anything to them.

"If I were a real minister, I would know what to do about a thing like this," Dr. Jellicoe censured himself. He was in such a brown study, he almost didn't see the little figure sunk into the shadows at the far lefthand corner of the auditorium, but as he was walking down the side aisle on the way back to the platform, he had a sudden impression of drowned violet eyes.

"Kathleen," he cried. "I am glad to see you."

"Oh, thank you, Dr. Jellicoe," Kathleen whispered. "I just had to come."

"Well, of course," Dr. Jellicoe assured her. "You should have."

He peered into her strained, unhappy face. The child was suffering over something. Once again the sense of his futility swamped him. He should have done something about Leonora before now.

Miss Smollett had come out on the rostrum and was walking across to the organ. Dr. Jellicoe hurried forward, not knowing exactly whether he was in a hurry to have it all over or whether he merely wanted to get a closer view of Miss Smollett in her soft, blue velveteen dress. She had a youthful flush on her face, and her eyes were deep and unfathomable. She looked like a Madonna, Dr. Jellicoe thought—the Christmas Madonna. Then he remembered that Miss Smollett was a spinster and, blushing, looked away.

Dr. Jellicoe's heart was like a rock in his breast, and his mind was busy with all his own and his flock's seemingly unanswerable problems when he raised his hand and said his simple prayer. Dr. Jellicoe couldn't say the things he wanted to—it would have taken all night. Somewhere, far above the little town of Chester, that understanding man who had forgathered with humans and known their foibles and failures, their perplexities and despairs, must have understood his unspoken thoughts.

When he had finished, the organ's mellow notes sounded, and the Angels' Chorus filed solemnly in. The archangels clambered upon the makeshift platform with only a few minor mishaps. The little-girl angels lined up in front of them. Out in front, somewhat removed from their fellows, in a little promotory of the rostrum, stood Evelyn McManus and Anna Cermak. The polished toes of Anna's little black shoes made the only dissenting note in the company of white innocence. The angels' faces, to a man, were frozen with quiet stage fright.

They made a beautiful picture, and the audience stirred restlessly in their seats, craned forward to pick out the most important angel or archangel in the lot—their particular angel. But something was wrong. There was too much strife and weariness in the room, too much struggle and defeat and worry. There was no satisfaction.

Dr. Jellicoe put his hand up to his head. He felt as if his heart would burst. Something had to happen. Something had to relieve this tension. Miss Smollett struck the pitch, and the organ dropped to its softest register. Just as the thin, piping voices of the children began to intone "Silent Night, Holy Night," something did happen.

A wild, barbaric noise originated in the basement, came screaming up the stairs into the rear door of the church and down the center aisle, accompanied by two hurtling white streaks.

Amazement froze the assemblage. Their eyes popped, but nobody moved a muscle, not even the Angels' Chorus. When people remembered it later it seemed as if the course of events followed the crazy pattern of a comic strip—one of those ridiculous inventions where one object touches another, and that in turn sets off another on down through a long string of idiotic consequences.

Jezebel was way out in front, but Whiskers, horizontal with speed, was closing in on her as she tore up the five steps to the platform and took sanctuary in the glistening Christmas tree, all claws bared, spitting and snarling, her back in a stiff arch, her tail aprickle. Whiskers, barking wildly, raced frantically round and round the base of the tree, knocked a box from under the makeshift platform, and tumbled the archangels to the stage. This set the whole tree to quivering, and at last one candle loosed itself from its moorings and went sailing through the air in a burning curve. It was the candle which Mrs. Brittain had affixed the previous morning just before her attack of faintness.

The immobile audience saw the flaming candle describe an arc and land squarely in the middle of the alligator cosmetic kit, on top of the hairbrush. The composition material burst instantaneously into a licking flame, just below the flimsy cheese-cloth dresses of the two smallest angels.

Panic followed. The screams of women tore through the air, and the people began to mill and scramble and trample each other. Dr. Jellicoe beat at the flames with his bare hands, without being able to stifle them. Mr. Philbert burst out of the pastor's study, snatching off his velvet coat as he ran. He threw this over the fire in an effort to smother it, but the flames had spread to the tissue-paper packages and were crackling around the whole platform. Dazedly Dr. Jellicoe heard the organ still playing and then the clear, high voice of Miss Smollett directing the children to form in line and march to the Sunday-school room. "And I mean it," Miss Smollett cried. "Don't look back."

The terrified Angels' Chorus did as they were bidden, all but two. The smallest angels stood perfectly still, like terrified ponies, mesmerized by the fire. Curtis McManus, struggling toward the aisle, was forced to stop and lift the inert body of his wife, Vera, onto a pew.

"Move back, Evie, move back," he shouted to his daughter. "Daddy's coming!"

But somebody was before him. Lunging through the crowd came big Joe Cermak, knocking people right and left with mighty swings of his great arms. A curtain of flames surrounded the platform, but Joe didn't stop. He swept through it, oblivious to burns, swung his powerful body up on the rostrum, and swept the children up in his mammoth grasp. For an instant his big body, a child under each arm, was silhouetted against the background of the giant fir, with fire all around his feet, like some great prehistoric creature; then he turned and stalked down the shallow steps, carrying the children like sacks of meal.

With the removal of the most immediate peril, Dr. Jellicoe turned his attention to the crowd. Half a dozen women had fainted, and their families were bent over them in frantic efforts of revival. Dr. Redding was moving among them with swiftness and dispatch, giving directions, and they were taking them. His earnest young face was flushed and grave, but in it there was a wistful look of happiness to be of use at last. There was a doctor in the house.

Mr. Dellinger was attempting to bring order out of chaos—standing on the platform steps, shouting orders, and giving advice—and people were listening to him gratefully. His twenty-five-year-old knowledge of the aches and pains, the prescriptions and potions of Chester gentry stood him in good stead.

"Go to Mr. Mason, Doc," he shouted to Dr. Redding. "He has a heart condition. Might keel over in the excitement."

"Hey, folks, don't run over Mrs. Willis. She's expecting."

"Get Grandpa Phelps to the window. This smoke'll be terrible for his asthma!"

Even Dr. Redding looked to him for instructions. He was an important man again. Still the panic went on and still the church remained full. Dr. Jellicoe saw a sweating knot about the storm door. They couldn't get it open. He raced down the aisle to the door. He knew its quirks.

"Don't raise a window," Mr. Dellinger was warning. "We can't afford a draft. One of you boys go down to the basement and crawl out through a window and get the fire department."

The fire was eating into the carpet now, and Mr. Philbert was running from the lavatory to the auditorium with a scrubbing bucket of water to dump inadequately on the fire. The mountain of Christmas presents was crackling higher and higher in leaping flames.

Dr. Jellicoe struggled with the door.

Inside the auditorium a great many odd things were happening. Everybody in the room seemed to take full blame for the conflagration.

"Oh, Curtis," Vera said weakly. "Whiskers started it all. It's our fault for not keeping him penned. Oh, what shall we do? To think what might have happened except for Mr. Cermak. Oh, Curtis, I'm so ashamed."

"It was my present that started it," Willie Turner moaned. "That's what I get—that's what I get! If I hadn't quarreled with Kathy . . ."

"Jezebel!" Kathleen was weeping. "She must have got out when I left. Oh, why did I ever come!"

"I told him to put it there, and I'm the one who opened up that case," Miss Smollett was thinking in the Sunday-school room, where the children were huddled. "If I hadn't been mooning around, I would have had more sense."

"I knew I never should have bought that darned alligator thing," Mr. Dellinger was repeating over and over.

"I might have realized this fire hazard," Dr. Jellicoe was saying through stiff lips. "I was too busy thinking about myself."

"Oh, Tom, I'm going to faint." Young Mrs. Brittain drooped against her husband's shoulder. It was the first conversation they had had in two days.

"Patty, what's the matter?" Tom pushed aside the tightly wedged crowd, got to her.

Then it came over Mrs. Brittain as clearly as if it had been an annunciaton—that moment of nausea and weakness on the stepladder, half a dozen things. "Tom, I think I'm going to have a baby," she sobbed.

"A baby!" shouted Tom Brittain. Nobody paid him the slightest attention. "But, Pat, that's wonderful!" He picked her up in his arms and kissed her. "Don't cry, darling."

"But it's all my fault—the fire," Patty mourned. "I would have candles—and then, yesterday, I got to feeling faint up there on the ladder, and I didn't get that one fastened good. That one that fell off! Ooooh. Suppose it had been our baby up there in that cheesecloth dress."

"But it wasn't!" Tom pointed out sensibly. "And you couldn't help it."

It was at this moment that Kathleen finally found Willie in a cloud of smoke.

"Willie," she cried, and threw herself in his arms, heedless of his mother, who was being fanned with a hymnbook. "Willie, I'll marry you. I don't care if she turns me out of the house. I love you, darling!"

"Kathy! What are you doing here? I was just feeling so good because you were out of this— safe."

"I'd rather be here—with you," Kathy said peacefully.

"Kathy," said Willie with a great sigh of relief. "I was so afraid I'd lost you." He choked on smoke and emotion.

"Dear God, please let me get this door open," prayed Dr. Jellicoe incoherently, "and I'll have it fixed tomorrow. I'll never neglect things again!"

All at once the door did open, swinging wide from the other side, and Miss Leonora stood there, glaring.

"Have you seen——" she began, and then caught sight of pandemonium, a scene which can only be described as a miniature replica of something by Dante.

"Oh, my goodness," exclaimed Miss Leonora, and set foot in the church for the first time in five years.

"Miss Leonora," Dr. Jellicoe quavered. "Don't

go in there. I can't allow you————"

Miss Leonora not only set foot in the church, wild horses wouldn't have kept her out.

"Is anybody hurt?" she shouted masterfully as she sailed down the aisle. A horrible clangor arose outside, and directly behind Miss Leonora hurtled the Chester fire department, wearing their red fire hats and dragging the Chester hose with its burnished brass nozzle. They made a strange procession.

Miss Leonora was apparently bound for the holocaust to put it out personally, but before she got there she found Ada Turner, stretched out in a pew, in a dead faint.

Miss Leonora didn't stop to reason why. She sat down and began to chafe Ada's hands.

"Put her feet higher than her head, Wilford," she advised the distracted Mr. Turner. "Ada's subject to fainting spells in moments of excitement."

"Ada, Ada," she said almost tearfully, "pull yourself together. We've got to get out of here."

Miss Leonora was so preoccupied that when she saw Willie Turner kissing Kathleen it didn't register.

The water was now pouring on the leaping flames and soaking the candle-lit Christmas tree, to which Jezebel was still clinging, moaning piteously. People who were able to gather their families together and get out the door were starting their cars to go home. The flames diminished as rapidly as they had begun, and Dr. Jellicoe noticed with sharp relief that in ten minutes they were reduced to smoking embers with nothing seriously damaged but the Christmas presents. These were a charred heap of rubbish. Not a present was intact.

From behind the Christmas tree, Santa Claus emerged, soaked to the skin, holding by the scruff of his neck a cowed and quivering Whiskers. Mr. Philbert had a broad grin on his face. There were always compensations. For one thing, that smoldering mess didn't include a beaver coat for Mrs. Philbert. The firemen put up a ladder and retrieved Jezebel from her lofty perch. When they handed her to Miss Leonora, that worthy took her absent-mindedly and said, "I'm so ashamed." But nobody knew whether of Jezebel or herself.

Joe Cermak had thrown open all the windows of the church and let the cold winter air rush into the smoke-filled auditorium. People began to revive on all sides and stop clutching their loved ones to them in death grips. The atmosphere was easier than it had been all evening—easier than it had been for years. The smoke-blackened, heat-singed faces were happy—happy and grateful and relieved. Families were reunited. Lovers were in each other's arms. Friends had come back to the fold of friendship. Snobbery had been wiped out, and envy and jealousy forgotten, under the stress of common peril.

The great weight in his chest which had been dragging Dr. Jellicoe down for a long time dissolved, and he felt free again—free and hopeful. He sensed this change in all his flock—as if the climax and violence had restored to them the use of all their faculties for kindness and understanding, as the maimed or the mute are sometimes restored by the pressure of events. He knew, without knowing why, that they had made a new beginning in Chester—that it was Christmas in the fact.

But something was still missing. Something important. His heart plummeted with terror. Miss Smollett! Where was she? Suppose she had been trampled, burned, overcome with smoke, knocked unconscious by the powerful stream of water. He couldn't remember when the organ had stopped playing. But the organ bench was empty. She was gone.

The thought was insufferable. Dr. Jellicoe raced blindly down the aisle, toward the rostrum.

"Dora! Dora!" he cried. He had never called her by her first name before. "Dora!" His voice rose hysterically, but everybody was too busy to pay the minister any mind.

Except Dora.

Miss Smollett was still in the Sunday-school room, trying to comfort the panic-stricken angels, when she heard her name called. Now she came through the door in her dress of old blue, the light streaming behind her, her hair ruffled into an aura about her head.

Dr. Jellicoe was stricken with her loveliness.

"Dora," he breathed, and just as he did so he caught his toe in the worn carpet and pitched forward once more.

"Ernest," Miss Smollett cried, and ran down the steps to him while he scrambled to his feet.

"Dora," Dr. Jellicoe said, wondering why he had never thought of it before. "Will you marry me?"

"Oh, Ernest," Dora answered, against all the advice of the live-alone-and-like-it books. "Do you want me?"

"Do I want you?" queried Dr. Jellicoe in a daze. "Don't you know I'm in love with you?"

The light of heaven burned in Dora's eyes.

Mr. Philbert had been going over the church to estimate the amount of damage. He came up and stood beside Dr. Jellicoe and Miss Smollett. "It's a miracle," he said, "how little damage was done. The church is not hurt at all—except for the boards around the rostrum and the carpet. We'll have to have a new carpet."

Dr. Jellicoe, rubbing his shin, could hardly forbear to sigh in relief.

"It's a miracle," Vera McManus said, "that no one was hurt or killed. We just don't realize how much we have to be thankful for." She hugged Evelyn to her.

Ada Turner and Miss Leonora Webb were walking out of the church arm in arm, as if five years of quarrelling had not intervened in their friendship.

"That's the miracle!" said Mr. Dellinger. "Would you look!"

All over the church Dr. Jellicoe heard the word. Miracle. He felt his skull begin to prickle. Three nights ago, Dr. Jellicoe had sat right here on this strip of torn carpet and said it would take a miracle. But miracles weren't like that—made out of the homely materials of a cat-and-dog fight. That was sacrilegious! Dr. Jellicoe put the presentiment right out of his mind. But it kept coming back, sticking up in his mental processes like a sore thumb. After all, there had been much about it that was miraculous! Who was he to question the method by which heaven translates its intimate changes to the earth? How did he know what miracles were made of?

Dr. Jellicoe pondered his secret, hugging it to himself. He didn't say anything. People might think he was crazy. But he believed in miracles. When he looked at Dora, he believed in miracles.

The firemen had stretched a rope around the charred area. They were going to stand guard to prevent a repetition of the fire. People were really beginning to go now. It was pleasant to hear their voices, not worried any more about trifles— knowing that trifles don't count. He listened to the diminishing crescendo of their talk.

"You and Kathy come over for dinner, now," Ada Turner was saying to Leonora. "Come about twelve. I've got lots to show you."

"Watch the step, darling," Tom Brittain

murmured. "You have to be careful now."

"Honey," Willie said to Kathleen, "I'm sorry your present got burned."

"My present!" Her voice lilted.

"Yes," Willie whispered. "It was what started the fire."

"Willie," Kathleen said, "did you buy that case for me?"

"Who else?"

"I thought—I thought maybe that Marcia Garrison——"

"She went back to Chicago," Willie said. "She went back to her husband. Anyhow, why would I buy her a present? Mrs. Mason asked me to be nice to her because she was unhappy."

"Oh, Willie! I've got your present here. I saved it for you."

"Merry Christmas, Mr. Cermak," Vera McManus said, "And we can never thank you——"

"It wasn't nothin'," Joe said.

"It was wonderful," said Curtis. "We'll never forget——"

"Will—will you let Anna come over and play with Evie? They're the same age——"

Dr. Jellicoe smiled. It was a miracle.

When they had all gone, Dr. Jellicoe put on his overcoat, and he and Miss Smollett stepped out on the walk. Overhead the sickle moon floated high and clear, and star shine was reflected on the snow. Dr. Jellicoe looked up at the delicate spire of St. John's, and his heart was very full. The church meant more to him than it had ever meant.

At the corner where he always turned off for the manse, he took Dora's arm, and then he tipped up her face in the starlight and kissed her.

"Ernest, somebody might see us," Dora rebuked him happily. "It's not customary . . ."

Dr. Jellicoe kissed her again.

"We're all through with what's customary in Chester," he said.

When he had left Dora at her door he walked back to the manse, trying to sort out impressions and make evaluations. All through his veins ran a strange, wild exhilaration. He stood a moment on the steps, looking up at the translucent sky. Dr. Jellicoe wouldn't have been the least bit surprised if it had suddenly split asunder and shown him the heavenly hosts singing Hosannah.

The little town of Chester was still and beautiful under the blurred blanket of snow. Over the sleeping houses, over the filigreed tower of the church, over the stone mansion with its guardian fir, over the shops and streets and byways, over every fence corner and road intersection and barn lot and chicken coop, over the soldier's monument in the square and the steep gables of the post office lay the benison of midnight quiet.

For a brief instant the dreamless hush was broken by the heartbroken whine of a lonely dog, banished from familiar territory to the confines of a chilly barn. The howls increased in volume and violence and then they stopped.

"Shhh, Whiskers," hissed Freddy McManus, and leaning down, he untied the rope that bound his friend, scooped him up in his arms, and reentered the house. Freddy tiptoed noiselessly up the stairs, his hand over Whiskers' nose, and into his own room again. Drawing back the covers, he thrust Whiskers into his forbidden bed and climbed in after him. With a profound sigh, the instrument of miracle pushed his wet muzzle into Freddy's hand, and boy and dog slept.

There had not been so much peace on earth or good will to men in Chester in more than a hundred years.

Inconstant
Star

Canada Butler, not being philosopher, king, or
keeper of any kind of flock, was more embar-
rassed than anything else when he saw the star in
the December dusk. It made him nervous, blazing in the winter sky, where it never had been
before, diminishing if not wiping out the constellations he had learned by rote. It spoiled his pitch,
and that was about all Canada had left. Wasn't it
bad enough to stand on a concrete island in the
middle of Times Square and hawk a telescope at
twenty-five cents a look, without having some
yokel ask you a question you couldn't answer?

From the beginning, Canada hadn't felt right
about the telescope. It had been a comedown for
him—not subtle enough for his talents—it was

like selling tickets for the merry-go-round. He
was no stranger to blue sky, but he'd never
thought to catch himself selling patches of it for a
quarter. Well, a man has to make concessions in
this world, do what he can get to do. When the
Little Marvel Touring Shows polished off the last
of the dusty county fairs and holed up in Linton,
Ohio, for the winter, Canada began to feel restless. He liked to keep moving, but the outlook for
a carnival man is not heartening anywhere when
the snow flies. He ought to be made like a bear, to
hibernate when winter comes on, because the
tired tinsel of his profession belongs to summer
starlight and the harvest moon. Nobody needs a
barker in December.

Towns like Linton depressed Canada. He had
come from such a town, where the oaks and
maples shed their leaves over low roof tops, and
hens scratched and clucked in the back yards, and
there was always a passel of kids and a pack of
dogs trotting around on aimless errands. They
turned off the lights and took in the sidewalks at
eight o'clock in Linton. Even the pool hall was
deserted, and there wasn't any place to go, unless
you counted the Chili Parlor, where some of the
carnival folks gathered to play checkers.
Checkers!

The girl situation wasn't promising, either.
There were plenty of girls, but they looked neat
and prim and innocent, as if they were still in high
school or had two-fisted steadies or husbands or

an old man who dropped his shoes meaningfully in the upstairs bedroom at nine o'clock.

Canada, who once had been the husband of a girl in Meadow Lakes, Minnesota, and the father of a baby girl, felt claustrophobia creeping over him in Linton, Ohio — a smothering sensation. When he saw people ambling home at dark or smelled somebody's dinner cooking, he wanted to cut and run, to get out of Linton and into a place where something exciting was happening.

There was also the matter of small change. It wouldn't have been sensible to ply any of his usual sideline trades in winter quarters where the chances of moving on were remote, and Canada never had been on friendly terms with manual labor. Let the weight-lifter hire out at the local coal and grain emporium as a coal heaver and the snake charmer measure ribbon in the notions store; Canada was dedicated to living by his wits. The day old man Bascom handed him a paint-brush and a bucket of red enamel and nodded toward the mud-splattered wagons, Canada made up his mind. He packed his things in his old canvas valise and headed for New York City.

He had a small stake—percentage of the summer take and result of a fortunate poker hand—but he rode in the day coach. In spite of posted warnings to beware of professional card sharps, Canada managed a few hours of successful seven-up with some downy service men and ran his money up to about $250. The future looked bright, because everybody knows there are more hicks in New York than anywhere else. Show them the shell game, and they'll buy it. It seemed to Canada he was now in a fair way to get rich.

After about twenty-four hours of being stunned by the overpowering masonry of the city and the turgidity of its streets, Canada decided to make some contacts. A mild-looking, moonfaced fellow he met in a pinball alley on Fifty-second Street was his first contact. His name was Bert, and he fleeced Canada out of his capital by one of the hoariest dodges known to the business. Canada, chagrined at finding himself a greenhorn in the Big Time, became not only poverty-stricken but wary. New York seemed to be slightly ahead of the medicine-show circuit.

Canada was reduced rapidly to guest of the city and began to take handouts from the brown monks on Thirty-third Street. The first snows were beginning to fall, and he hadn't even the fifty cents requisite for a flophouse at night. Sleeping in the subway or a railroad station got less and less restful. There was work to be had but Canada had no liking for the bonds of business. He was lonely for the pitch, for the circle of eager faces, slack-mouthed, wide-eyed, bent on him with tense concentration, for the build-up and the pay-off when he played on the crowd as if it were an instrument, and the crescendo of falling silver.

Step a little closer, folks! Draw in. Right over here, sister. Would you let the lady through, sir? I

want everybody to get a good chance to see our
splendid offering, because I haven't got the words
to describe it, folks. I'd have to be a regular poet.
Yes I would! Get away, boy! Now, folks, for only
ten cents, one tenth of a dollar, a measly little thin
dime, two buffalo nickels, ten copper cents,
folks—

But Canada lacked the splendid offering. The
war had been hard on the handy can openers and
shoddy knives with which you could whittle potatoes into useless daisies, make curls of simple
carrots and fringe of honest celery. Nobody
imported those wizened roots from China, which,
if you put them in water and let them stay six
months, might sprout a few woody tentacles of
green and might not—but by that time you would
be far away. Even the magic hair lotions (*Will*
make curls out of the straightest hair!) and the
tonic elixirs (*Good for every ill of man or beast!*)
had disappeared.

Canada was lonesome and homesick. But how
can a man who is homeless be homesick? Canada
asked himself, and he tried to think back twenty
years to Meadow Lakes, Minnesota, where he had
sold groceries for Ephraim Bros. and gone home
at night to a four-room house and a wife called
Dorothy and a baby they had named Marjorie.
Dorothy had brown hair and soft eyes, and the
baby was fat and comical. The house was bare,
but Dorothy had fixed it up with rag rugs and cur-
tains and sewed some patchwork quilts for bed-

spreads. He remembered one Christmas she made a tree, tugged an evergreen from the woods and decked it with strings of popcorn and those paper chains kids make in school.

The baby's white sock had looked little and funny hanging there by the old black stove—funny and pitiful. It was enough to break a man.

But mostly it seemed to him Dorothy had been trying to get him to do something he didn't want to do, like fix the gate, and the baby had squalled a lot.

It couldn't be Meadow Lakes he was homesick for. He had left it without a qualm. He remembered that night when Dorothy said she simply had to have some money, the baby needed a coat before winter set in, and had he ordered the cordwood, and for heaven's sake couldn't he do something about the front door, which was sagging and wouldn't lock? It was raining, and wet diapers were hanging on a rope behind the kitchen stove, and Dorothy had a cold. To get out of the house, he went to the drugstore to buy a package of cigarettes, and while he was lounging around there, his month's pay heavy in his pocket, the night express came through, bound for Minneapolis. For no reason especially clear to him, he got on it.

He was one of those men who never come back from a nocturnal walk to the drugstore, but disappear and find themselves a new, if no more satisfactory, life. Of all the men who, in the slough of domesticity, sometimes consider such rashness,

Canada was one of the few who escaped.

At first he had some fantastic notion of getting rich quickly and returning in splendor to reclaim his wife and child. But the path to easy riches was no more navigable to Canada than it is to stronger characters, and his years were spent on the downward path. When an ordinary man would have given up hope and after a few bouts with questionable oil stock and and phony gold-mining certificates would have gone back to work, Canada still followed the gleam.

He sold everything from bogus stocks and bonds and racing tips to hula performances, and though he had lived, he could not be said to have prospered. As the years ran by, his ability to associate himself with Big-Time operators diminished and he deteriorated into a barker. He was still the handsomest barker on the small-town circuits, and his voice had all the come-hither of a Pied Piper's.

Inevitably the memory of Meadow Lakes had dimmed, until he was hardly able to conjure up the outlines of it or to fancy himself among its citizenry. The twinges he at first experienced concerning the plight of Dorothy lessened, until in his memory her face was merely a blur.

No, it couldn't be Meadow Lakes he was homesick for, Canada thought; but his malaise was genuine, and it occurred to him that if he had a home, it was the carnival. But his last carnival, hunkered down now in Linton, was as remote from him as the moon. If he started out to hitch, he never could make it by Christmas. Besides, Canada hated exercise.

It was quite by accident that he ran into Pearl McCready, the wife of one of his old friends from the Peerless Midway Associates—a group he had traveled with more than ten years before. Joel McCready had had a marvelous racket—all he had done was let people look through a giant telescope he had acquired in a shady deal with a pawnbroker, charge so much a look, and speak some gibberish about the constellations. The people had eaten it up. They had loved it. And more than once Canada Butler had envied him his livelihood.

Asking immediately after his old friend, Canada learned from Pearl McCready that he was dead—killed six months before by a truck he thought he could bluff out of a right of way. And the giant telescope was dead, too, so far as Pearl McCready, widow, was concerned. She had not yet got around to selling it, but she was through with midways—already she was going steady with a restaurateur, who owned a place on Ninth Avenue. Why didn't Canada take on the telescope? Obviously Canada wasn't doing anything now. Sure, take it over, the book *Simplified Astronomy* and all, and pay her when he got around to it.

Canada guessed quickly that this generous gesture was simply a means Pearl McCready had for salving her conscience—by giving the telescope to one of Joel's old pals, she needn't feel so bad about forgetting Joel in such a hurry and getting hitched to a city bloke. So Canada had no compunction about accepting the deal, and it was arranged without a thought on his part of ever paying.

His first night on Times Square was a great success. He set up the telescope on the island that supported the bronze statue of Father Duffy at the intersection of Broadway and Seventh Avenue, and out of the the rivers of people a sufficient number paused to stand and listen to Canada's impassioned advertising of the heavenly bodies.

The ring of bemused faces, surrounding him once more, hanging on his words, drove him to flights of oratory; and the public was soon standing in line. Canada, who hardly had mastered the mechanical adjustment of the telescope, gave them brief looks at the sky, only slightly magnified by the cheap lenses of the instruments, and briefer lectures on the constellations, which he still could not locate with or without the telescope.

Airily he asked every woman her birth date and then identified her with any star he could see through the telescope. When he observed with what avidity they listened, he raised the price from ten cents to twenty-five. At midnight he had ten dollars.

Canada was stunned. He retrieved his valise

from a locker in Pennsylvania Station, got himself a hotel room, and had ham and eggs for breakfast the next morning. Later in the day he had a cardboard sign painted: "Professor C. Butler, Astronomer. Learn the Secrets of the Heavens." He bought a white shirt and black knit tie and began to take on an academic demeanor.

Meanwhile, the Christmas multitudes swarmed in the Square, mushing the sooty snow underfoot, jostling one another in the high fettle of holiday cheer. The animated signs twinkled and glowed. The mammoth head on a cigarette billboard puffed artificial smoke rings toward the Astor Hotel; ridiculous showers of glycerin bubbles drifted heavenward from a soap advertisement; steam escaped from a cup of neon coffee. The roar and grind of traffic competed with the blare of carols from radio amplifiers.

Canada, who never had looked higher than the clock on top of the Paramount Building, found himself staring into the depths of the cold, pure sky of a winter's night and wondering. He hardly had looked at the sky since he'd left Minnesota; but now, as he gazed at the infinite meadows of heaven, he began to have a curious feeling that somewhere in it a sign was set for him. He didn't like it. It gave him the creeps.

He was surprised at how pretty things looked up there, almost the way he remembered they looked in Meadow Lakes when he was a boy courting Dorothy. He recalled one night when they were in her father's sleigh, with the bells ringing in the thin, light air, and it seemed to him the stars were hanging down on stems, right over his head. The telescope reminded him of that. And the night Marjorie was born. He didn't know what to do with himself. He went out in the below-zero weather and stood there, gritting his teeth and looking at heaven and making demanding prayers.

One night a little past the middle of December, Canada was standing on his Times Square island about seven-thirty, whistling as he waited for the crowds that soon would assemble. Absently he adjusted the telescope and squinted into it. He drew back and looked again. In the circumscribed circle of the lens, on a field of midnight blue, there blazed a golden thing. Canada shook his head, then glued his eye to the telescope, for he supposed he was suffering from hallucination. But it was still there, serene and golden, bigger and brighter than any star he ever had seen. "Where'd that come from?" he muttered, and began to thumb through his astronomy book. In the indifferent light he could not find a map that included such a spectacular heavenly body. He blinked and looked to the northwest with his naked eyes; but there was not a glimmer of golden light, and the fixed constellations moved on in their accustomed courses.

"Well, I'll be hanged!" Canada said.

At first he felt unreasonably elated. This would wow them—a brand-new star at Christmas, sailing northwest of Times Square. Wait until he got that into the spiel! But when he opened his mouth to announce his discovery, he changed his mind. A small, cold chill ran down his back, and he didn't want to say anything about it. Who was he to say there was a new star above the confused and weary world at Christmas? He didn't know anything about it. He'd better keep quiet.

People had begun to press around the telescope. Canada launched his pitch, but his heart wasn't in it. As he droned on he found that he was worrying. "Somebody is going to ask me about what it is or what it means," he thought. "And I don't know."

"Twenty-five cents for a look through this powerful telescope," he ended. "Only a quarter, the fourth part of a dollar, to learn the secrets of the heavenly bodies."

The crowd surged up. He adjusted the telescope, moved the sights down, and held his breath. As he swung it around, he waited for their outcries, but nothing happened. They paid their money, and they took their glimpses, and they went away satisfied and unmoved. Canada stared at them. He couldn't believe it. He wished they would go home so he himself could look through the telescope. But business was wonderful. Long after midnight they were still coming up. At last there was only a kid left, a boy about sixteen, and

Canada was so shaken that he let the boy fool with the sights and swing the telescope on its pivot.

Finally he said "Say, bub, do you see a kind of bright gold star over there—sort of to the northwest?"

The boy swung the instrument around and pointed it to the northwest. "Nope."

"Look again," Canada said. "Here, let me fix the sights." Then, "Now, right over there."

"I don't see anything."

Canada shrugged. "Okay," he said.

As the boy moved off, Canada squinted through the lens. There it swam, radiant in its field of blue, refracting long rays.

"I must be losing my mind," Canada thought. "If it's there, anybody ought to be able to see it—they couldn't help it. If it's not there, how can I see it?"

He folded the telescope and scuttled toward the hotel. He felt peculiar. Once before there had been a star not everybody saw, or at least a star not many people paid the proper attention.

"But a thing like that couldn't happen to a man like me," Canada scoffed. "Not educated or smart or important. I don't know anything, and I don't amount to anything. I'm not even honest."

Having made this remarkable admission, Canada was struck by a bolt of remorse that kept him sleepless. Crowds of people he had cheated rose up around him in his small hotel room and looked at him with trusting faces. It was their looks of trust that undid him. He would have preferred these phantom faces to be distorted with menace or anger or hatred. But they looked kind and confident. Somewhere among them were the faces of Dorothy and the baby, and he had to shake himself to remember that the baby wasn't a baby any more. She must be about nineteen years old. So the whole thing was silly.

As he alternately paced the floor and tossed and turned in his bed, it seemed to him that he must begin to make restitution for the means he had taken of earning a livelihood. Otherwise he might never get to sleep. He thought of Dorothy and the baby; but it was so long ago, and perhaps the kindest thing he ever had done had been to leave Dorothy. Maybe she had figured out a decent life for herself, and Marjorie probably didn't know that her father was a carnival barker. Maybe she was in college, and if she found out, it would embarrass her. He wondered what she looked like—whether she was blond like him or dark like her mother—and if she were tall and if she were happy.

But he couldn't start there. He had waited too long. If you begin at the beginning, you never finish. On the other hand, if you begin at the end and work back, you might get there someday before you died.

After that night Canada approached the telescope gingerly, as if it might be alive or an instrument of the devil. But it was inanimate and cold. Not knowing what else to do with himself, he set it up at the accustomed stand, determined not to look into it. But the urge to see whether or not the new star was still there overcame him, and he adjusted the lens and looked. Serene and golden, the star floated in the circumscribed circle. Canada shut his eyes. He shut his mind, too, and began to warm up to his pitch; but he couldn't come out with it. Somewhere between yesterday and today he had lost his knack. His voice was hoarse and he couldn't think of anything to say. Trade fell off, and most of the time Canada stood by his telescope like a wooden Indian, not saying anything, just waiting for destiny to overtake him.

He was relieved that a heavy snowfall obscured the sky the following night, and he stayed in his room. Feverishly he looked through astronomy charts for some hint of his find; but nothing explained it. When he had finished his research, he sat with his head in his hands, wondering what he ought to do.

A week dragged by in this manner, and Canada began to lose weight. He did not seem to be in command of his life, but at the mercy of unknown direction, and he dreaded for day to break or night to fall. It would have been in keeping with his character to take to his heels. It had been his life-long method to run when the going got heavy; but an iron will, not recognizable as his, seemed to have welded him to Times Square.

When the snow stopped and the skies cleared, he automatically dragged himself to his stand and set up the telescope and his sign. He took a first look. The large star winked back at him. He shuddered down his long, brawny length and decided he had taken leave of his senses. He stood silently beside the telescope, waiting for somebody to notice it. A few people sauntered over, and a man with two children, a boy and a girl, bought each child a look. Canada rumbled out his lecture, but the fire was gone from him. The little girl clung to her father's hand, and Canada found himself affected by the sight. He felt like crying and was afraid he might do some such fool thing.

He didn't know why the sight of a little girl clinging to her father's hand should so impress him. She was a prissy kid, with yellow pigtails and two front teeth missing, not what you'd call pretty. But it was something about the way she hung onto her old man, leaned against him and impeded his walk, and the look on her face when she turned her head up to him—a kind of he-belongs-to-me look. Marjorie hadn't been big enough to hang onto Canada's hand; but if he had stayed around, one day she might have put her little paw in his and looked at him like that.

That was really what he wanted, Canada thought. Somebody to look at him as if he mattered.

But it was too late now. Marjorie wasn't a kid any more. He hoped suddenly that Marjorie was having a wonderful life—a sort of heaven-on-earth life. He hoped she had a good home, and lovely clothes to wear, and a young man she loved who soon would begin to devote himself to her forever. It was the nearest Canada ever had come to prayer.

"I can't stand it," Canada moaned. "I can't stand any more of it."

It was a bitter night, and the crowd thinned early; but still he stayed there. Now and then he took a fearful look at the imperturbable thing that had become the center of his limited universe. The wind howled coldly around the corners, and his fingers were almost too stiff to adjust the tele-scope sights; but he waited. A superstitious notion had come into his head that he must wait—that something important was about to happen.

Around one o'clock in the morning a man and a girl came across the vacant street to Canada's island, and they stood there shivering, waiting for the traffic light to change. Canada studied the girl's face —young and shallow and a little fright-ened. She had a floss of light, silky hair, which blew about in the cold wind, and her shabby reefer covered some kind of party dress, a poor red thing with rhinestones on the skirt. She wasn't wearing gloves, and Canada surmised that she hadn't a pair that matched her dress and pride had sent her out bare-handed. On her thin wrist was a cheap and sparkling bracelet. He yearned toward her, as someone a little like himself a long time ago, someone who loved bright, sparkling things and because she couldn't get real things was willing to settle for imitations. She looked about twenty.

The man with her was more than twice her age. "About my age," Canada thought. "Old enough to be her father!" He was a thick-chested, dark man, a bit too sleek, and he wore a well-cut overcoat and a good soft hat, but his face was mean. It was an ugly face with hard eyes.

"Robbing the cradle!" Canada muttered with new piety, and the girl turned and looked at him with her wide blue eyes.

"Oh, look, Ed," she said. "It's a telescope—for looking at the stars."

"Who wants to look at the stars?"

"I do, Ed. Please, Ed," she said.

"Come on, baby. I'll show you some stars," the man said.

Canada was outraged. He almost forgot his troubles in his distrust of this situation. The girl looked at him with silent pleading, as if she wanted to delay their progress and was using him as an excuse. He saw that she was frightened. He had to do something.

In the empty square he began to pitch. It all came back to him unbidden. His voice soared on the still air, ingratiating, coaxing, magnetizing.

Ed was impressed in spite of himself. "Okay," he said to the girl.

She bent her light head and fitted the telescope

to her eye. Canada began his lecture tonelessly, swiveling the instrument for her as he talked.

"Oh, what's that one?" she interrupted. "That big gold one over there?"

"Where?" Canada demanded, his hair rising.

"Over there!" she said. "To the northwest. It's wonderful."

"Do you see it too?" Canada whispered.

She straightened up and looked at him in astonishment. "Well, of course! It blots out everything else."

"Honest?" Canada said. "You can see it? Well, maybe the only people who see it are the ones who need to see it!"

"Look, Ed," she said.

"Aw, come on, come on!" the man said. "Let's get going. What are you trying to do—freeze me to death?" He reached for her arm.

"Let her look!" Canada said mildly. "Let her get her money's worth."

"You keep out of this," Ed said.

The girl's face was white and beseeching, and Canada stared at it. Then he unlimbered his muscles and said to the man, "Take your hands off her!"

"Shut up," said Ed.

Canada whipped out his wallet and peeled off a bill. "Here, kid," he said. "Take this and run. You ought to be able to get a cab in front of the Astor. Go home and stay there. Haven't you got enough sense to know what you're out with? Now beat it!"

Patiently Canada removed Ed's hand from the girl's coat sleeve and gave her a push. She fled, like a scudding leaf, over the snow, running like a child, not looking back.

Ed wasted no time. He charged Canada and landed the first blow. As Canada's chin went up, everything became lucid to him. He knew everything he had missed, thrown away, lost, despoiled, and squandered—the things that might have been and never had been, the things that had been and might not come again. Joyfully he swung his big fist.

For a while there were only powerful grunts and the thuds of blows in the silence, and then the empty street came alive and black figures raced from every direction. There was the shrill squeal of a policeman's whistle. Canada heard it dimly, wishing they would let him alone. He was slugging as he hadn't slugged since he was a kid, and he was being punched as he never had been punched. Blood was running down his cheek, and one eye felt peculiar. The fellow knew how to fight, and if Ed hadn't got his legs entangled in the telescope, nobody knows how the whole thing would have ended. They fell with a crash, and Canada found himself sitting on the chest of his enemy. The telescope was shattered beyond repair.

When the police roared up, Canada was grinning with his cut mouth. "Well, I got him," he proclaimed. "He was pestering a kid!"

Ed bellowed protest, but the police took him away. Canada was complimented for his quick action. Nobody suggested that he, too, should climb into the police wagon. He was treated like a responsible citizen, on the side of law and order. It was a new experience. They were even solicitous about his wounds.

"Oh, it's nothing. Nothing at all," Canada said.

He leaned over with conscious dignity and gathered up the broken bits of the telescope. Then he carried them back to his hotel. They seemed to deserve some kind of decent burial. When he packed his canvas bag he put them in the bottom. There was no longer any reason for him to stay in New York. Whatever urge had bound him was dissipated. It was still four days until Christmas, and if he started at once, he might be able to make it.

When the morning train for Chicago pulled out, Canada Butler was on it. He didn't know exactly where he was going, but he thought it might be Meadow Lakes, Minnesota. Anyhow, he was on his way.

As the train started its long trek up the Hudson River, a careless hand in the basement of a church on Riverside Drive flipped off the airplane beacon light that shone yellow on top of the Gothic spire. But that didn't make any impression on Canada Butler. He didn't even know it was there.

The
White Kid
Gloves

The dictionary defines happiness as good luck, prosperity, a state of well-being, and whenever I read this accepted description, it interests me to remember that the moment of utter happiness I cherish out of a lifetime was attended by no one of these things. On the contrary, luck had been so long absent as to become a total stranger, prosperity was not even around the most distant corner, and I was running a low fever.

The winter that I was sixteen, my father suffered a series of paralyzing business reverses owing to circumstances he could not control. He was the owner of a small, independent organization which he had founded and built into a comfortable position, and he loved it with the devotion of a man who understands responsibility and appreciates work. A series of misadventures, which began in the middle of the year, culminated in October with the default of a note he had signed for a friend in cheerful confidence, and he was forced to pay out of his working capital the sum of $25,000, which was about the total of it. He found that he was literally penniless and that eventual recovery lay months, even years, in the future, if at all. The times were inflationary, and almost the bitterest pill to swallow was the fact that prosperity flourished on all sides but eschewed his path. He had established a standard of living commensurate with his prospects, which included a pleasant house with a sizable mortgage, a wife he loved to indulge, and two expensive and slightly spoiled children, Stanley and me.

My father was not a man to burden his family with business worries, and during the early days of his travail he brooded in silence on the downward path of his fortunes. As the number of his employees diminished and then vanished altogether and his working hours increased, he was forced to take my mother into his confidence. I do not know to what extent she was frightened by his revelations, for she never gave an overt sign, past dispensing with the maid of all work and the yard man, and her assumption of the full role of cook and houseworker—with my brother and me as her assistants, positions which did not fill us with enthusiasm.

While I fretted at the ironing board and my brother grumbled as he stoked the furnace and raked the autumn leaves, my mother sang at her work, and my father summoned a kind of haunted cheer in our presence. It was only after we had been driven upstairs to attack our homework that the burden of unease seeped through the house. I would lean over the banister in the dark and observe my parents clinging together on the sofa as if they occupied a bit of driftwood in a raging ocean, and pick up bits and pieces of their conversation . . . the low, murmurous undertones of distress.

"But, Whit, could you sell the business?"

"I don't know. I suppose so—at a loss."

"It would relieve you of a burden. You could always get a job."

"That might solve things. Gebhardt would take me on. Or I think so."

"But you don't really want to sell it, do you?"

"No, I believe in it—if we can weather this spell."

"I believe in it, too," my mother would cry loyally. "We'll find a way. Now, you're not to worry about it another minute!"

My father would smile warmly.

The dominion of money over human beings is a devastating thing. It is, as everybody knows, inedible and of no real use in building a fire, and in any elemental situation it is worse than useless, but in the limits of our society too much can be a dagger and too little a bludgeon. I do not suppose that my father and mother ever thought we should actually go hungry or cold, but they knew that the quarterly note on the house mortgage would roll around inevitably, along with the insurance premiums and the taxes and the fuel bills and the grocery accounts, and that credit and honor are inseparable. I had not the experience at the time to know how their minds ran around in tortured circles, like frightened squirrels caught in a maze, but I have since had reason to discover.

"I don't know how to tell you this, Eloise," my father said one night, as he stood before the fireplace, drumming his whitened knuckles on the mantel and looking away from her. "I've taken a job."

"You've decided to give up the business," she said, her voice gray with defeat.

"No," he said. "I'm on the night shift at the Eldorado Hotel—night clerk. Would you like a room, lady, single bed?"

"But, Whit," my mother cried, "you can't work day and night!"

"You underestimate me," he answered. "And I expected a more passionate protest."

"Oh, Whit," moaned my mother, "how can you joke about it!" and began to cry.

My father enfolded her in his arms and nuzzled her hair. "Now don't blubber," he ordered. "You know I can't stand a crying woman."

She continued to cry.

"Your eyes are beginning to look like shrimps," he told her, "and your nose is swelling. I should think you would consider your looks on our last evening together."

She moaned afresh. "You'll wake the children, sweetheart," he chided. "And anyway, it's only temporary. Just think, they're going to pay me regularly."

My mother took a dim view of a regular stipend. "It's too lonely," she wailed.

"I'm here," he reminded her. "And time's wasting."

I scuttled up from the landing as they began to turn out the lights. My cheeks were hot with shame. My father—working in a cheap hotel. I didn't know anybody whose father was a night clerk. It was mean and horrid, something I could not admit to my friends. I felt very rebellious.

If life had been uneasy heretofore, after my father began his double duty it became more so. He used to stumble home at 6 A.M. and fall into bed until noon, then eat lunch and set out for his empty office. He did not come home at dinnertime, and my brother and I rarely saw him except on Saturday and Sunday mornings, when we were not in school. He looked very tired and cross, and we missed his joking and his teasing. We missed him, but my mother was as one bereft. She pursued a program of the stiff upper lip when we were in earshot, and most of the time she was certainly too busy to mope, but during the long winter evenings I can remember her attacking the darning as if each raveled sock were a bitter enemy, staring out the window into the night, or looking around our pleasant living room with its mellow chintzes and books, deep sofa and rosy fire, as if she might never see it again.

Christmas had always been a halcyon time for us. My father loved it as he loved all bright and charming things—the flowing eggnog bowl and the people who came to call, the red satin ribbons and the mystery of packages, the turkey to be carved and the salads mixed, surprise and affection and gestures. They were part of his nature. He set store by tradition, and his Christmas trees were a marvel of taste and originality, though he was very bad in the electrical province, and the strings of lights were always going off and reducing him to profanity.

My mother had a warm heart for Christmas, too, and in that season her bustling hostess-ship reached its finest flower. From my earliest childhood I could remember the rows of cakes—the fresh coconut and the children's cake, a tower of splendid white icing bristling with little colored candies, the plummy dark fruitcakes and the chocolate layer; the mince and apple pies; the homemade fudge and divinity candy; the popcorn balls and the candy apples. The house was always rife with delicious smells—baking fowl and spice and the scent of drying spruce. The doorbell never stopped ringing. But the doorbell gets less busy in troubled times.

As Christmas came on, general nervousness around the house increased. Nobody mentioned it, and Stanley and I waited in vain for some cheering word.

"I want a bike," Stan said. "Ed Miller's got a bike. Garry's going to get a bike. I've got to have a bike."

"I don't think we can afford it," I said, from the store of intelligence I had harvested eavesdropping. "I think we're poor."

"Are we?" my brother asked anxiously. "Who told you?"

"Nobody, I just think so."

"We still go to the movies," he pointed out.

"But *they* don't," I said meaningfully. "They don't want us to be deprived."

"What's that?"

"Well—not to have things."

"Then they must want me to have a bike," Stanley said. "If I had one I could get a paper route. Then I could make money." Stan was always ready with a rationalization.

"I want something pretty," I said. "Something not practical."

"Like what?"

"Like a party dress with a long skirt and a pair of white kid gloves."

"Aaah. You're not going to any party."

"I am too. I'm going to Ruthie's Christmas

dance, but I won't go in a short dress without gloves."

"Who wants an old pair of gloves?" said Stan. "I want a bike. But don't tell anybody."

We had long solemn conferences about how we could dispel the pall from the household. I thought of marrying a rich old man and lifting the mortgage, since I had been busy reading trashy novels. Stan saw himself winning an air race and bringing home a bag of gold and presenting it to my father. None of these schemes seemed to lead to any practical solution of the problem of getting money for Christmas shopping. We had one enthusiastic notion which depended upon selling our school books to the secondhand store, an idea which seemed to have everything except that we should certainly be found out.

Time flowed into December. The busy merchandising season, replete with emerald and scarlet trappings, department-store chimes, draggled wreaths, and pseudo Santa Clauses, broke over us, and still nobody said anything. My mother had a haunted look, as if she were waiting for my father to speak, and he seemed impervious to the brash advance guard of the Yule. We began to feel both betrayed and dogged. The bicycle and the white kid gloves ceased to be desires and became causes with us. We whined aloud, though it made my mother cringe. We complained at our housework.

"Maybe it isn't coming this year," I said at last,

banging the pots and pans about after dinner.

"What isn't coming?" my mother asked.

"Christmas," I cried.

"Christmas always comes for people who have the right spirit."

"Not to us!"

"Christmas comes in your heart."

"But not like last year," I wailed. "Nothing's the same any more. Nothing." I began to sniffle, and rushed up to my room, where I sobbed on the bed, luxuriating in self-pity.

She followed me and voiced the immemorial platitudes. "The real joy of life is giving—not getting," my mother said. "You probably won't believe me now, but you'll find out."

"But that's just it," I wept. "I want to give too, but I haven't anything to buy it with. I haven't any money!"

"Darling, I haven't either," my mother said sadly. "You're a grown girl. You'll have to find your own way. Please don't mention this to your father."

"I never see him, anyway."

"No more do I. And I'm afraid it's harder on me than on you. Now wash your face."

"I'll show them," I muttered after she left me.

Thereafter I was sullen and fierce, and my pride was bedraggled. Surreptitiously I had applied for a job in the school cafeteria, not as a waitress but as a dishwasher, since I could not bear the thought of moving among my schoolmates collecting their soiled trays. I made my way to the steamy kitchen after my last class by various subterfuges and lied out of after-school strolls and sodas with uncompromising duplicity. I did not much mind the job, though it was tiresome work, but with youthful snobbery despised the thought of stigma.

Only my ability to weave any incident into the fantasies of an overactive imagination made it bearable. To myself, during this period, I was all the heroines of history, but I still smelled to myself of steam and suds. For my munificent effort I was paid two dollars per week, and since Christmas was three weeks away I could not hope for more than six dollars. Nobody knew about this venture. I could not bring myself to tell even Stan.

I didn't see much of Stan, anyway. I got home late and Stan was usually gone. Sometimes my mother was gone. The whole close-knit structure of our household seemed to have fallen apart. We were all silent and secretive, and when we were together we did not find anything to talk about. My mother's eyes pleaded with me, but I held myself stiffly away from her. My father made wistful little jokes at Sunday-morning breakfast, but I would frown instead of laugh. It did not occur to me that night clerking was as hard for him as dishwashing for me. Inside me there was a dark bruise engendered by what seemed his neglect.

Only Stan was normal.

"I'm making *him* a pipe rack," Stan said to me. "In manual training."

"But he doesn't smoke a pipe," I objected.

"I guess he would if he had one," said Stan. "I figure to get one to go with it."

"How?"

"I'm going to trade my knife," he said. "I know a guy who's got a pipe that's nearly new."

"What about *her*?"

"I'm making her a little box," Stan said, looking proud. "I'm carving her initials on it. She can put her beads and stuff in it. It's a real strong box."

I thought warmly of my four dollars buried in the bureau drawer among my pictures of movie stars. I had spent it a hundred times and stretched it a thousand ways until it had become a fortune.

Christmas came on Wednesday that year. The Sunday before, my father came downstairs haggard but cheerful. His step was full of bounce, and his eyes were bright. I did not know until years later that he had finally scraped enough cash together to pay the interest and the installments on the house and we were sheltered for another six months.

"Well, I'm taking the day off," he announced. "To gather the Christmas greens. Who would like to accompany me on a search for a Christmas tree?"

"They're so expensive this year, Whit," my mother protested. "Don't you think we're all old enough to get along without?"

"Nonsense," said my father with his old authority. "Never too old for a Christmas tree. Besides, we have received a gift. Mr. Feeneman, an elderly guest at the Eldorado Hotel, has given me permission to raid his wood lot. In the spirit of our ancestors, we will obtain a tree by dint of the ringing ax."

I loved to hear my father talk when he was in his historical mood, and the thought of a Christmas tree broke up the ice in my bosom. My heart lightened and Stan squirmed with excitement. As an added boon, my mother said she would remain behind and put the house to rights so that we could get an early start. Dishwashing by now had become anathema, and to be spared any session of it was more to be desired than rubies.

We set off through a light snow, already coating the earth, for Mr. Feeneman's wood lot, which turned out to be four miles in the country. My father made hearty comments upon the wholesome value of winter exercise, though I think this was to camouflage our lack of carfare. As we trudged, he pointed out the various trees to us and told us their Latin names. Awed by his unfailing erudition, I panted after his long steps, though I was tired enough to faint and the snow was running down my collar.

The cold wind began to blow more bitterly. Stan's teeth chattered, and my father's face began to look pinched. When we at last arrived at Feeneman's wood lot it was the most unprepossessing acre of scraggy, leafless trees and brambles, without an evergreen shrub in sight. Just like the wood lot of any guest of the Eldorado Hotel, I thought in rage. We went over it miscroscopically, and when we were just giving up Stan raised a shout from the farthest corner, and we rushed there to find a lopsided little cedar, ravaged by wind and weather, gnarled, frazzled, and old before its time. I thought it looked awful, but my father pronounced it prime. He unsheathed Stan's Boy Scout hatchet and began to chop.

The tree was very tough and my father was an inept woodsman. About halfway through the proceedings, a chip flew off the trunk and smacked Stanley in the eye. He yelled like an Indian and began to dance about in pain. My father was sick with self-disgust and misery, and I was soundly frightened. The blood ran down Stan's cheek and he bent himself double to stop his own outcry.

"We must get him to the doctor," my father said.

"No, no," Stan wailed. "We have to finish chopping."

"It doesn't matter about the tree," my father quavered. "Your eyes are the most important thing!"

"It doesn't hurt," Stanley bellowed, mopping at the gore with his sleeve. "I can see out of it. And it *does* matter about the Christmas tree. I want a Christmas tree," he babbled, like a baby.

My father was in a frenzy of indecision, and while he traveled in circles, Stan seized the hatchet and finished chopping down the cedar— the blood from the cut above his eye staining the snow.

"Oh, my God," Father croaked. "Come here, boy. I must bandage up that thing."

He examined the eye, which was swelling and turning plum color, and bound up Stanley's head in his white linen handkerchief. This turned out to be a minor blessing, as a farmer in an old car, witnessing the miserable tableau, drew up by the side of the road and took us in, Stanley still clutching the pathetic cedar as we huddled together on the back seat, the cedar needles prickling through our clothing. I began to sneeze and my father divided worried glances between Stanley and me. His face was long, and I suppose he was thinking that nothing would ever turn out right again.

We hurtled up to our door and staggered out. Stanley was shaken but cheerful. I was having trouble with my nose, and my father looked as if a feather would knock him flat. While he paused to give his thanks to our samaritan and wish him the compliments of the season, Stan and I dragged the cedar to the door.

My mother came out and stared speechless at our woebegone looks.

"Madame," said my father, "I have given your

son a mouse."

"Stanley," she shrieked, and Stan began to cry for the first time.

That evening we trimmed the Christmas tree. Nothing could disguise the fact that it was a dingy little cedar, not shaped to bear the lovely loot of Christmas, but it was the finest Christmas tree I ever saw. Stan was so proud of it, and as he bent his abrasions, contusions, and bruises above it, while he and my father affixed the stand, the light of happiness gleamed from his good eye. Through some inexplicable stroke on my father's part the lights all burned brightly, and as I sat stringing the garlands of popcorn and cranberries, and my mother tied on the cherished old baubles of a dozen childhood Christmases, it seemed to me that our mutual estrangement had vanished and we were a family again, safe from the world's alarms. This enabled me to ignore partially the fact that my throat was getting more sore by the minute.

By morning, my tonsils seemed to have closed off my windpipe almost entirely, but I did not mention it. It was my last day in the cafeteria, and I had to have the other two dollars. I took my accumulated wealth with me and after school I went shopping. The stores were crowded and I felt very warm and light-headed. As I began to hunt for the things I had imagined buying, I soon discovered the inadequacy of six dollars. One by one I discarded my dreams, but I could not quite give up the thirst for luxury, and instead of the warm woolen socks my father needed I came home with a pair of fine black silk ones, embroidered with a clock. Though my mother could have done with a pair of stout gloves, I chose a ruffly nightgown of some sleazy pink stuff, since it was what I would have wanted. For Stanley, I got a bicycle bell, knowing full well he hadn't got a bicycle, but it seemed to me that if you could not have what your heart desired, a bit of its music would be better than nothing. As I say, I was light-headed.

On Christmas Eve, I felt really dreadful. My throat ached, along with my head and all the other bones in my body, and my stomach kept turning over to add to the general dismay, so that I could not share in the frenzied celebration which marked the arrival of a twenty-pound turkey from Uncle Robert's farm. The very presence of the traditional meat seemed to buoy Mother and to make her feel that the times were back in joint, while Stanley and my father responded to the thought of something besides chopped meat; but I was not hungry.

I wished for nothing so much as to lie still in bed and not even think, but this was out of the question, as the bubble and squeak of Christmas now rose to crescendo. I alternated between chills and burning and resorted often to the bathroom for gargle and first aid, to retch or douse my aching head with cold water from the tap. Between chores I repaired to my bedroom to admire my offerings and try to persuade myself to wrap them up. When I had time I thought of Ruth's party, which I still had some hope of attending, having assured myself if worst came to worst I would wear my mother's old black dinner dress. In my fevered state this possibility seemed quite likely to me, though it never could have happened.

The day passed in a wave of hysteria, punctuated with nausea inspired by the delicious smells which came from the kitchen–the old smells of Christmas. In spite of my indisposition I felt cheerful. The house had come to life again and was full of happy secrets, bustle, and normalcy, and if the Christmas tree bore no tangible fruit, still it was there, setting its seal upon the season. My mother's moodiness had vanished and her voice had its ring of maternal authority. Stan, his face piebald in the yellow and mauve of bruise, bore his scars like a soldier and seemed to have turned overnight from a nagging little brother into a man. My father had been whistling when he left the house.

According to our custom, the Christmas tree was scheduled for the night of Christmas Eve. My father had got the night off from the Eldorado. When I came into the room in the late afternoon, Stan was laying the fire on the hearth. Three forlorn little packages, wrapped up by Stanley in scraps of ribbon and string, were disposed under its scrubby branches. I arranged my three around them.

"I guess that's all," I said hoarsely.

"I guess so," Stan mused. "I hope you like what I got you."

"I will."

"You want me to tell you what it is?" he asked eagerly.

"No, no! I want to be surprised, I have to be surprised!" I cried out with passion.

"I wasn't going to tell you, anyway," he said, grinning on the unbruised side of his face.

At dinner I could not eat.

"She's too excited," my mother said. "She can't take anything calmly. Look at that flush. She looks as if she had a fever."

I shrank from the tentative hand she put out to explore my brow.

My father leaned over and, putting his fore-finger under my chin, he tipped up my hot face and looked into my burning eyes.

"My little girl," he said, "is turning into a beauty."

The effect of his almost forgotten tenderness was to send a shiver down me, and I had to rush out of the room to stop the blinding tears. My love for him ached like a tooth. The lump of anxiety and worry and fear of the months past got mixed up in my sore throat and everything hurt terribly,

all at the same time. I could not keep from wishing I were dead, a natural emotion at sixteen when
the possibility is remote.

By the time I had regained composure the
inevitable dishes had to be washed, but I was
almost grateful to have something to occupy me
until eight o'clock. I offered to let Stan off from
the drying to be alone, for I was afraid another
word would send me flying into little pieces, but
gallantly he insisted, not to be outdone in
generosity.

Embarrassment fell on Stan and me in the
kitchen. Our friendship was deep and lasting, but
neither of us could talk about it, so we did not
talk. We hung about in the kitchen after we had
finished, not knowing what to do with ourselves.
Then we heard my mother at the piano and my
father's sweet, true voice, singing snatches of
"Silent Night." The year before we had raced like
little children, but now we walked sedately, and
Stan stood back and let me go in first.

The fire blazed and the room was soft with
candlelight from the stubby storm candles set in
the old brass candelabra. The little red and green
bulbs glowed like jeweled fruit on the cedar tree.
A snowfall of packages piled around the base and
to one side, refracting the firelight, stood the
gleaming bicycle. Stan's mouth dropped and I
thought, with almost my first pure unselfishness,
that I would rather he had got it than to have anything myself.

It is impossible to say more about the intimacy of the scene which ensued. It happens multiplied millions of times in this season, and you had best remember your own time. The happy cry which leaps from a young girl's lips when she draws from its tissue wrappings her first long party dress, even if it be fashioned from her mother's last taffeta negligee, is an old story. Surely you too have unwrapped your first pair of long white kid gloves with the dear little buttons at the wrist—the beautiful, delicate, white kid gloves which mean that you are a grown woman, forever above the soil of childhood.

It was late when we settled back from the charged emotions of exchanging gifts to sip the mulled cider. Stan was in a stupor of pleasure, swathed in his new sweater my mother had knitted up in the school colors, and assaulting our ears with the brassy twang of the bicycle bell. My father was already wearing his new shoes (my mother's present), and his old ones, lined with the gray soles cut from old laundry boards to keep the damp from the holes, stood grotesquely under the Christmas tree. He was smoking the pipe that had been smoked only a time or two before and coughing, while he fondled his silk socks, his face alive with awareness that they were the best money could buy. My mother had put on her pink nightgown over her dress, and it became her. She sat tracing the initials of her name, which Stan had carved into the box top, with gentle pride. I stroked my treasures alternately. I could not keep from touching what I loved. Stan had made me a fan and it was the crowning fillip of frivolity.

"Why, it's midnight," my mother said, aghast. "It's been a long day. Run along to bed."

A slight contretemps followed, which could be solved only by permitting Stanley to take his bicycle upstairs with him. He swore he could not be parted from it overnight. I then persisted that I must try on my dress and gloves and show them off. A strange leniency had descended upon our parents. These things were permitted.

I stood before the mirror in my room, slipping the amethyst taffeta over my head, which continued to feel dizzy. It had a low neck which showed the smooth curve of my shoulder, and the live color reflected in my eyes. I swished the skirt and I caught up my long white gloves and swept out of the room in an exaggerated copy of my favorite movie heroine. I touched the hair at the back of my neck tentatively and smiled an enigmatic smile. I paused on the landing in my made-over finery, drawing on a glove. All my senses responded to the sibilance of silk and the satiny softness of the glove against my bare arm. As I peered in the dark, enjoying the rash décolletage of the dress and the unaccustomed flow of skirt around my ankles, I leaned over the banister in a last excess of childish eavesdropping.

My father and mother were standing before the hearth. I saw how stooped his shoulders were and the new frost on his dark hair.

"Whitney," my mother said in a voice of happy puzzlement, "however did you do it—the bicycle, the gloves . . ."

"I don't blame you, Ellie, for thinking I've been at the Eldorado's till. It looks too foolish for our busted economy. But it was luck, honey, the Barton luck!" He summoned a grin. "So help me, I won the bike on a punchboard at the Rexall Drugstore. I went in there the other night to get a cup of coffee and a doughnut, and there was one hole left in the board. What did I have to lose but a cup of coffee?"

"Oh, Whit!" she cried. "You went hungry."

"Just a tinhorn gambler," my father said. "But you've got to take a chance now and then!"

"But the gloves—"

"Well, I saved five dollars. I've been walking home from the hotel. Need a breath of air after an all-night stretch, you know."

My mother didn't speak.

"I had luck again," he said. "There were a bunch of measly-looking gloves on a table marked 'clearance,' and right down in one corner was this pair—just what the doctor ordered—and dirt cheap!"

"They're beautiful! You've made them both so happy."

"When you're sixteen," my father said, "or just twelve, you deserve to be happy And when you're an old man, you can't bear it if now and then—at

Christmas, say—you can't make wishes come true. You can't bear it, Ellie, being a failure to your children!"

"Don't say a thing like that. They've never wanted for anything in their lives!"

"But it's not enough—food and shelter and advice. You've got to give them something else, some kind of symbol of what the world can hold—something to reach for. Anyway," said my father, his voice trailing off into a whisper, "my luck didn't last."

"You can only have so much luck, Whit," my mother said.

He faced her, and his face was broken up and he swallowed painfully. "I haven't got anything for you, Ellie," he said. "I bought you a bottle of that stuff you like—that lilac stuff, whatcha-macallit? But I got tangled up in the damn bicycle chain and fell down. Lord help me, I broke it!"

His despair was comic, and the picture of my debonair father entwined in the chain of Stan's new bike was funny enough to tickle anybody. I wanted to giggle and I waited for my mother's laugh.

But she didn't laugh. She turned toward him so that her full face was to me, and such radiance burned on it, such an indescribable expression of pride and fulfillment, of faith and hope and love, that I was forced to drop my eyes.

"I love you," she said. "I'd rather be married to you than any man alive!"

They were motionless, two figures in a frieze, immobilized by the force of mutual feeling. They moved at the same time, without volition, melted together, entwined, touching—man and woman, but one entity.

It was then that my moment of happiness broke over me in brilliant, prismatic splendor. All finite things dissolved, the horizons of the earth rolled back, the firmament immeasurably deepened, and I could hear that strange music which falls upon the inner ear only a few times in a life. All the voices of all the angels sang in my head, and every beat of every heart. I knew that the secret of life was almost in my grasp. I looked up the long arches of the years, and they beckoned. I leaned toward the future, abandoning fear. I was dizzy with my untrammeled ability to see what cannot be seen with the physical eye, to see beyond the little limitations of the human orb into the extensions of the spirit. I turned upon my infinite pinnacle and saw them far below—the two loving figures who had given me the secret. How small they were and far away, and how my heart surged toward them. My father had straightened up and was standing tall, and my mother's laughter now spilled out. From my eminence I knew that they were invincible as long as they had breath, and even after. I did not doubt it for a moment.

In this eternity which occupied only a second in time, I had continued to tug at my other glove without knowing it. Now I drew it off and looked at it and pulled at the fingers to smooth them. Then I turned and went back upstairs. I could not intrude further on what I had witnessed, and I did not want to see anybody. I wanted to be alone and remember what I was waiting for.

On Christmas morning I had a high fever, and thickly over my swollen face the rash had materialized. The doctor, summoned from his own Christmas, sniffed at the door, and almost before he had looked at me he made the diagnosis. "Measles," he said. "Fine thing for a great strapping girl! And a fine time to have the measles!"

But nothing could touch me. I could not even regret too deeply the loss of the Christmas party. I was quite happy to lie in the dark and ponder my thoughts.

There was compensation in the measles, for if I had had to go to the Christmas party, my father would have discovered what he never in all his life knew. Both of the white kid gloves he had struggled to buy were for the left hand.

The Poor
Black Sheep

There are people who are simply born with a champagne appetite and a beer pocketbook, and the roads they travel are graded by these circumstances, along with the terrain of their environments and the people who travel with them. But the wish that exceeds the grasp lies behind all their doings.

Of this school came both Daniel Morgan (better known to the public prints and a good many files and dossiers as Danny Deever) and Fletcher Bassett, who, up until last Christmas, had never got his name in the paper. They were small-town boys, and their early days did not differ radically. They both hung around the Corner Drugstore in Wayland, Missouri, with the usual aggregation of loafers who accumulate in such places. The chief difference in their activities at the time was that, while Fletcher divided his time between swabbing the soda fountain with a wet towel and delivering Doc Clancy's prescriptions on his bicycle, Daniel inclined toward the alley, where he shot craps with pool hall characters, or he stood in front of the plate glass windows, ogling the high school girls.

They were both dreamers. Their dreams were similar in that they were concerned with wealth and power. Daniel's dealt with penthouses, a low-slung Cadillac (maroon), loud suits (tailored), sharp shoes (handmade), girls (beautiful and without too many clothes), and other ingredients of gracious living. Fletcher's had to do with industry (of which he was a captain), a two-story house (pillared and drenched with magnolias), sons and daughters (half a dozen assorted), and Kathleen Fane. The boys could scarcely wait to get grown and accomplish these fantasies. As has been noted, the basic difference in their philosophies was that, whereas it never occurred to Daniel Morgan that it would be necessary to work, it never occurred to Fletcher Bassett to do anything else.

Having virtually nothing in common, they were great friends. To humble, rotund Fletcher, Daniel Morgan was alter ego—a tall, narrow boy, with eyes the color of quicksilver, a dark brush of hair, thin, restless hands, and a look of supercilious arrogance that quelled any detractor. Fletcher was squat and freckled, with a lank mane and beseeching blue eyes. In their friendship, his was the role of inordinate admirer and willing slave. It was Daniel who planned their adventures, bold and brassy, and Fletcher who executed them and took the blame. Still, it was Daniel who lent to Fletcher's humdrum existence the color of excitement, and there existed between them a kind of rough affection that neither was likely to forget.

Both had eyes for the same girl, Kathleen Fane, a pretty, dimpled piece with red curls and eyes like deep, autumnal pools. In Wayland's meager aristocracy, she was the highest-born lady. She lived at the edge of town in an ugly brown mansion of many cupolas, gables, and verandas. Her father was too aristocratic to work. He had always subsisted on income, which, along with his plantation acres, had now virtually disappeared. He was actually as poor as Father Morgan, a hard-pressed carpenter, or Fletcher's sire, who owned the local butcher shop.

It was proof of their brotherhood and the sheer hopelessness of conquest that Daniel and Fletcher were able to share this damsel in their imaginations without jealousy and to despise with youthful vigor a more favored suitor—Arthur Patterson, a pasty-faced student at Yale, who was the son of A. P. Patterson, the president of the Wayland State Bank. There was nothing about Arthur that pleased the two friends, and if the truth had been known, there was little about him that pleased Kathleen. Arthur bored her almost as consistently as he bored Daniel and Fletcher, but the necessity of being squired by him whenever he was in Wayland was a family responsibility. Mr. Fane and Mr. Patterson were lifelong associates, conservatives, Republicans, deplorers of what went on in the modern world, and viewers-with-alarm of what might happen next. They had long since decided to join the aristocracy and money of Wayland and keep it in two families.

Kathleen was a dreamer too. The stringency of her life in the moody, rococo house offered little else in the way of amusement. She dreamed of great occasions (parties and balls), of raiment (court gowns with ruffles and trains), of blazing jewels (diamonds), and men (pining away for the love of her or sweeping her off her feet, leading her out in the waltz, or kissing her on the neck). Both Fletcher and Daniel entered into these hallucinations, but Arthur, never.

Wayland offered little to feed such burning imaginations, but on Christmas Eve, when Kathleen was sixteen, she was taken to the Elks Club Cotillion by Arthur Patterson. She was wearing a rose-sprigged challis frock, run up by loving hands at home, and her mother's coral necklace, but the wild-rose damask of her cheek and the mahogany of her piled-up curls owed no homage to any lady of fashion. She was as beautiful as a spirited redheaded girl of sixteen can be once in her life. Arthur was virtually stupefied.

Fletcher, whose only hope of gazing on the scene of enchantment represented by the Elks Club Cotillion lay in serving the ice cream at midnight, had willingly accepted the assignment. When he stared through the crack in the kitchen door and saw Kathleen being whirled around the floor, he went dizzy. But Daniel (in a presentable dinner jacket—his possession of which was a mystery), whose presence in the hall was without formal invitation, let his eyes rove over her bare shoulders and was inspired to action. He sauntered out on the floor in the middle of a program dance, an unprecedented effrontery, and touched Arthur's shoulder.

"May I cut in?" he inquired.

Arthur frowned at this display of vulgarity, but before he could protest he felt Kathleen dissolve from his grasp. She moved off with the barbarian, and there was nothing he could do.

"I love the way you dance, Danny," she said in his ear.

"I love you," stammered Daniel, unable to summon embellishments from his meager vocabulary of love.

"You mustn't say such things," Kathleen reproved in a manner that invited him to continue.

"Come outside with me," Daniel whispered urgently, partly because he wanted to be alone with her, but also because he had noted that the stewards of the club were consulting the roster of invited guests where, undoubtedly, they would not find his name.

"Oh, I couldn't, Dan," said Kathleen as they moved toward the corridor that gave on the kitchen.

"Wait here," he commanded, and pushed her down to a seat near the stairway. He went into the kitchen, where Fletcher, in a white butcher's apron, was polishing glasses.

"Do me a favor, Fletch," he said. "Get Kathleen's coat from the cloakroom. She has a headache—wants to go home."

Fletcher departed on his errand and came back with the coat, his pudding face full of concern. "I'd like to go with you," he said worriedly. "But I can't leave."

"I'll manage," Daniel assured him. "Carry on, boy."

They went out into the crystal night. Kathleen was quaking, but there was that witchery in Daniel that persuaded people against their judgment.

There is no logic for the way the mood of Christmas deepens the sky and revises the ordinary landscape. It was such a night as visits the earth no more than once a year. The leafless elms cast the dry-point etchings of their shadows on the snowy walks, and every house was eaved with spun sugar. The Confederate soldier, shouldering his stone musket in the center of the square, had a band of ermine on the visor of his cap. The little houses of the little town, so interminably dreary at other seasons of the year, now took on the outlines of happy fantasy. Their yellow lights blinked friendliness, and every doorway was brave in wreath and ribbon. The sentinel fir on the lawn of Judge Andrews' place had blossomed an electric star, and the town clock, announcing the inexorable hour, chimed a different music.

As they walked along, the grip of their mutual embarrassment dissolved. She leaned against him, dismissing all her qualms about Arthur and the heresy of having departed the Elks Cotillion before supper, giving herself over to the consideration of the spangles and pinwheels that bloomed in her head when he touched her. He was invincible. All the things he had ever wanted seemed almost to be his simply because, with such a girl, he could not fail. For such a girl he would loot the very earth and bring her all its plunder.

"I wish tomorrow would never come," she said, voicing the most hackneyed example of the things women say when they fall in love.

He was enchanted with the depths of her philosophy. "Me too," he said, though he knew that everything worth living for lay in the future.

He kissed her as they stood in the lee of the Presbyterian Church, and she held onto him. They sat down on the stone steps in the shadows and exchanged their well-worn dreams, when they got around to talking.

When Doc Clancy opened the store the day after Christmas, he observed that a flagon of *Nuit de Noël* was missing from the perfume case. He knew that he had been robbed, but it was not until rumors got around that the bottle had turned up anonymously among Kathleen Fane's Christmas gifts that he went to Fletcher's father.

"I hate to accuse the boy," Doc Clancy said, "but nobody else has a key to the store. I wouldn't mention it except it's for his good. You know that, Bass."

Mr. Bassett, in righteous dudgeon, demanded an accounting of Fletcher.

"I didn't take it," Fletcher said stubbornly.

"Don't lie to me in addition to stealing," thundered Mr. Bassett. "I'll tan your hide proper. You'll work it out, every cent of it, do you hear me? If you didn't take it, who did?"

"I don't know," said Fletcher. "But I'll work it out."

"Maybe I was hasty," Doc Clancy put in. "I think the boy's honest. I don't want him to work it out if he didn't take it."

"I'll work it out," said Fletcher. "But I don't want to hear any more about it."

A week or two later a blizzard swooped down on Wayland, and in the course of it Doc Clancy discovered that the skylight in the roof of the store was leaking snow. As he pulled down the iron ladder that led to the roof, he had a sudden inkling about the bottle of *Nuit de Noël*.

Somebody had been on the roof before him, and recently.

He went downstairs and apologized to Fletcher. "Some sneak thief came in here Christmas Eve and swiped that perfume," he said. "Up the ladder and through the skylight into the store. I'm sorry I accused you, Fletcher. I've got a notion now who the real culprit is."

"I said I'd work it out," Fletcher answered stoically, "and I will—whoever it was that took that perfume doesn't matter now."

"But that's silly, son. I've done you an injury, and I want to put it right."

"I don't want to hear any more about it," Fletcher said in an anguished voice. "Just don't say anything to anybody, please."

Doc Clancy shook his head.

In the morning Daniel Morgan was gone. Also missing was the sum of $106.82, painfully accumulated in nickels and dimes for the uniforming of the Wayland High School Band for competition in the state contest. Because he was the best-looking and the most suave member of the senior class they had elected him drum major and treasurer.

Daniel's father, a deacon, was able to pay back this money, in small sums over a long period of months, but not in time for the competition. When he recovered from his shock and first grief, he reacted in the best Victorian tradition. He swore publicly that if his son ever put in an appearance in Wayland again, he would beat him within an inch of his life, and he forbade his wife to communicate with her erring progeny as long as they both should live.

Kathleen, already in disgrace for the affair of the Elks Club Cotillion, had her reputation picked clean as a bone by the gossips and was confined to quarters by her father. Here she cried until her face was sodden, and then revived somewhat, as women will. But Fletcher—Fletcher was bereft of motivation and purpose. There was no one to comfort him. As he rode frenziedly about, delivering medicine during the influenza epidemic, the tears sometimes froze on his sandy lashes.

The emotions of Daniel Morgan on the subject were never known. He must have had some regrets—for his mother, with whom he had a certain rapport, for Kathleen, whose yielding mouth and soft eyes he never forgot—and for Fletcher. Old Dog Tray. And then, too, he never got to wear the white serge uniform with the golden epaulets and the bearskin shako and prance at the head of the parade, throwing his gilded baton into the pure, bucolic air.

But Wayland had no penthouses; the only Cadillac was an elderly model that belonged to A. P. Patterson; and the girls, even Kathleen, were awfully demure.

A few months after he arrived in Chicago Daniel was haled into juvenile court for having pinched a silk shirt from a Loop haberdashery. He had discovered the Arlington Race Track and had found that the methods that enabled him to cadge ice cream sodas from high school girls worked just as well with the more sophisticated daughter of an influential meatpacker.

He had seen her at the ten-dollar window collecting a bet, and when she turned toward him the look in his odd gray eyes so unsettled the girl that she dropped her bag. Lipstick, compact, handkerchief, car keys, and something over a hundred dollars flew in every direction. Daniel stooped to retrieve them.

He returned everything except a twenty-dollar bill, which stuck to his palm.

"I can't tell you how grateful I am," the girl said, stuffing her belongings helter-skelter into the alligator pouch without bothering to count the money. "I'm so clumsy."

"You were jostled," he said piously. "You can't be too careful at the track, you know. It's alive with pickpockets."

"Oh," she said.

"Let me see you back to your friends."

"That's very good of you." At the entrance she looked at him softly and said, "Won't you come in and have a drink? I know Daddy would want to thank you."

He exhibited a decent reticence. It was possible that when she sat down at the table she might decide to count her money.

"I was just leaving," he said. "I have an appointment in town. Will you be here tomorrow?"

"At the ten-dollar window," she said happily. "Good-by and thank you."

"Thank you," said Daniel, fondling the twenty in his pocket.

He was not at the ten-dollar window the next day. He was unavoidably detained. He had spent the twenty dollars for a pair of pointed shoes, but the silk shirt had been lying there.

It might have been better if the judge of the juvenile court had not been a woman. Judge Edna Gale was a specialist in youthful delinquency, but the boy fooled her. The pathos of the expensive shoes and the shabby suit and the fact that he had taken a pleated white shirt touched her immoderately. She was a plain woman, with dragged-back hair, but the wistfulness of her youth suddenly flashed over her, and she found she could understand the yearning for luxury that had made the hand go out and seize it where it lay.

She let him off with a lecture and presented him with a ticket to Wayland, a name she had extracted from him in her questioning. He thanked her with his usual courtesy and left for the railroad station, where he converted the ticket into cash.

Before winter came around again he had got mixed up with a gang of small-time gamblers and thieves on the South Side, and he had stolen a car.

Daniel spent his eighteenth Christmas Eve

sawing wood on a detention farm. His hands were blistered, and he had no stomach for the benison of turkey, supplied by a forgiving state. The next time he was brought to justice he was no longer a juvenile. He was twenty-two and a candidate for Joliet. He had added a gun to his equipment, and he got three years.

In Joliet, two things happened. He learned a trade and he made contacts. He was taught the elements of safecracking by an expert—an old lifer who had nothing much else to amuse him. Safecracking by means of manipulating the combinations of safes is virtually a lost art. Harry Case, who had been a successful burglar of the old school (before fate caught up with him, and he murdered a night watchman in a getaway) had a burning wish to keep the art alive. Next to him in the dining hall was a likely prospect— a moody young man with long, delicate fingers. Even in the most brief and transient of conversations—snatched words and far-apart hypothetical demonstrations—it was possible to communicate quite a bit of this information over a couple of years.

Together with this journeyman instruction, Daniel made a connection with a member of the Corriden crowd, a second-rate, small-time mob, who was serving out a rap. When he emerged from prison (having got ten months off for good behavior, and because, as a trusty, he had waited tables in the warden's quarters and come to the attention of the warden's wife) he had friends, of a sort, waiting for him.

During the next decade Daniel Morgan disappeared. He was transformed into Danny Deever, a moniker pinned on him by police reporters, out of an old Kipling ballad. He was a high-style thief who specialized in cracking the vaults of resort hotels where the big jewels usually accumulated —Palm Beach, White Sulphur, Southampton, Newport, Del Monte—and of the better jewelry houses and rich private homes in the United States and Europe. A neat operator, he was able to pilfer a wall safe in a great private house without leaving a print on the carpet or disturbing the petals of the roses that stood in a vase beside the area of his operations. The Corriden gang fenced the merchandise, dismantled it, and converted it into folding money. With this specialist in their ranks, the Corridens prospered and were able to afford the expensive legal talent, professional bondsmen, and other business attributes of a going concern. It was to the interest of Julius Corriden to keep the goose who kept laying diamond eggs out of jail. He went to considerable expense and trouble to do so.

Danny, by living dangerously, began to accomplish most of the material ambitions of his youth. He had a penthouse with a zebra-skin sofa, a white velvet rug, and some genuine Chinese antiques, a taste acquired in his nocturnal visits to the wall safes of houses on Fifth Avenue,

Lakeshore Drive, and Beverly Hills. He had also a Cadillac (bulletproof), suits of fine English tweed (more muted than his early visions, but tailor-made), russet shoes (created to his measure), and a mistress who never wore too many clothes.

It was true that his freedom was hampered; that he had to submit to the stupid direction of Julius Corriden one way or another; that he paid various types of tribute to bigger operators in the underworld; that he frequently had a nagging pain in his left shoulder—the souvenir of an improperly doctored bullet wound; that, in spite of the fact that he was guarded by a large, dull bruiser named Shark, he was usually afraid.

But there were occasions when he sat down to breakfast in his penthouse, in a pure-silk purple robe with his initials appliqued on it in gold, when Lily had not yet arisen to remind him of what she was and what he really was, that he got glimmers of the lost vision. He remembered that he had twenty suits, a dozen pairs of shoes, and a whole chest filled with pleated white shirts, but then he also remembered that he hadn't much of any place to wear them.

It had not come out the way he had planned, he thought. He had meant to go back to Wayland, drive around in his Cadillac, marry Kathleen Fane, and show them. But when these childish fantasies brushed across his mind in the midst of a sleepless night he would laugh out loud. Wayland, for God's sake! Who wanted to go back to Wayland, that one-horse Podunk of the prairies? How could Wayland still be in a world that also included Biarritz and Palm Springs and Mexico, D.F., and Rome and Nassau? Danny grunted. Whatever brought up the subject of Wayland? He hadn't thought of it in fifteen years.

He began to develop a phobia about the place. They say criminals always go home once before they die.

In that winter of his discontent Danny Deever began to get very jumpy. He went off his feed and onto the bottle, and he began to hesitate when a job came up. In his business this was fatal, but he couldn't overcome it. He was past thirty—old in his trade—and he was convinced that his luck was running out. He dreamed of vultures swooping when he slept, and he never slept without Seconal. Lily began to irritate him, and he struck her once when he was in his cups.

Julius was deeply concerned. Argument was of no avail, and Julius began to hunt around for something to snap his star performer out of the doldrums. Finally he happened on a piece of information that seemed made to order—a little, quiet, riskless job in Wayland, Missouri.

Danny, shaken to the soles of his handmade shoes, sent word that the answer was no. He was all but hysterical. Then Julius, accompanied by his usual quota of brooding colleagues with trigger fingers, dropped in one afternoon.

"Are you off your rocker?" Julius demanded,

regarding the dram of thirty-year-old scotch he was cradling in his fat fist. "This is a two-bit thing! A kid could handle it—an amateur. What's the matter with you? Getting tired of money?"

"There ain't no money in Wayland," said Danny. "I been there."

"You don't keep up. Senator Patterson inherited oil. Millions. He struck more. Cattle, land, real estate. He's rolling."

"For the rich the birds sing," Danny said lugubriously. "I guess I don't keep up. What d'ye know—old A.P.! I thought he was dead."

"Don't you ever read the papers?" Julius inquired. "Senator *Arthur* Patterson. He's no older than you are."

"That jerk!" Danny cried. "How'd he ever get to be a senator?"

"I guess it was when you was away," Julius said delicately, referring to a period when Danny had been too hot for the United States.

"Well," said Danny, "why do you have to go to Missouri to hunt money?"

"I never said money," Julius returned. "I was talking about the Empress necklace—that mess of blue-white diamonds you hear so much about. Senator Patterson just bought it for seventy-five grand."

"Yeah?" said Danny. "Always showing off, Arthur."

"It's going to be a Christmas present to his wife."

"Well, she deserves something—having to live with him."

"They're spending Christmas in the old homestead in Wayland. He's going to surprise her with it on Christmas morning, my scratch sheet says."

"Neat but not gaudy," ruminated Danny. "How are you planning to unload this crate of ice? Every individual stone has got its picture in all the museums, not to mention the Encyclopedia Britannica."

"I ain't planning to unload it," Julius said, "My Angie's took a fancy to it."

"Ain't that sweet!"

"I'm a sentimental man," Julius said. "I aim to give this Empress thing to Angela for Christmas. What's good enough for a senator's dame is good enough for Angie."

"Holy God!" Danny swore. "Go buy her a necklace."

"She don't want just any necklace," said Julius. "And like I said, I'm sentimental."

"Send somebody else," Danny said irritably. "The deal's too crummy for me."

"You ain't sneering at ten G's, are you?" Julius asked softly. One way or another he had to get this boy back in business.

"Are you kidding?"

"Remember who you're talking to," Julius snapped.

"I ain't hungry," Danny said. "I said send somebody else. I ain't in the mood for traveling on Christmas Eve. Going to hang up my stocking right here."

Julius' hand sought the inside of his coat. The colleagues automatically moved in. Lily twisted on a red satin chair. "I said you," Julius rasped.

Lily began to cry. "Don't go, Dan," she begged. "I got a feeling—"

Danny's mind had been occupied temporarily with a picture of himself and Kathleen on the steps of the Presbyterian Church. "Shut up!" he shouted. "Where is the damn thing?" he asked Julius. "In the old Patterson house?"

Julius relaxed. "The senator's leaving it overnight for safekeeping in the vault of some rube jewelry store—Acme Jewelry. You know where that is?"

"Yeah," said Danny. "Same building as old Doc Clancy's Corner Drug, if it hasn't moved."

"Well, Christmas morning, my information says, Patterson goes down there to pick it up and give his wife a big surprise. They leave that evening for Washington. All you got to do is blow down and twist a couple knobs—get back in time for me to give it to Angie when she wakes up on Christmas—around five in the afternoon."

"That's all?" Danny said sardonically.

"Can that! It's like candy from the baby, I tell you. Worst can happen is you tangle with a couple of hick cops."

"You wouldn't know," Danny said. "You couldn't know."

Julius laid five crisp one-thousand-dollar bills on the coffee table. "Earnest money," he said. "See you at the Picayune Christmas morning. Have a little celebration."

"You said ten," Danny pointed out.

"You got a nerve," Julius said. "Since when am I paying you anything in advance?"

"That's what I can't understand," Danny said.

"I wouldn't want to disappoint Angie," Julius said coldly. "And I wouldn't want you to disappoint me. Like I said, this is earnest money."

"Okay, okay." Danny succumbed wearily. Julius took his colleagues and his departure.

"Dan," Lily cried, and flung herself around his neck. "Don't go down there. I got a feeling it's a fix!"

"Aw, cut out your whining," he said as he disengaged her. "You been wanting a mink coat."

"I don't want it any more," Lily said. "I'll go tell Shark."

"Tell him nothing. I'm going alone."

"No, no!" Lily wailed. "I'm going with you, then."

He looked her up and down and threw back his head and roared with unattractive laughter. "You!" he said. "That's a panic."

If only the past could actually be destroyed, if you didn't have to think and remember. On the road back to Wayland he tried to make his mind a blank. But their faces recurred to him. His mother and father, long dead; Fletcher—old

Puddin'head—where had he got to? And Kathleen, whose kiss was like a drink of cold well water.

He reconstructed the Main Street of Wayland in his mind, and it was some time before he remembered the iron ladder that led to the roof of the one-story building and the skylights that gave on the Corner Drug, the Acme Jewelry, and the Montgomery Dry Goods. He had once had occasion to use this entrance, and it seemed logical to use it again.

He drove into Wayland shortly after midnight. It looked even smaller than he had remembered, and it was quieter than the grave. The wan light from the mackerel sky picked out the stone image of the Confederate soldier in the square, and the dim shadow of the Presbyterian Church steeple lay on the light snow that mantled the lawns and drifted down the roof tops. There was no one to be seen, only the phantoms of his memory, and their innocence and peace stabbed him like a sword of moonlight. He shivered, not from cold, and before he could get control of himself he saw that he had driven through Wayland and come out on the other side. If I was smart, I'd just keep going, he thought, and cursing, he reversed the car and went back.

He drove aimlessly around, past the house where he had been born—a sagging cottage that had deteriorated into something resembling a kennel. Then, without being able to stop himself, he took the meandering road to the east of town, past the brown monstrosity that had once seemed so grand to him. He threw his light on a sign that hung on the ornamental iron fence and read: "Wayland Funeral Parlor." His teeth chattered. I'm getting morbid, he thought, and decided against further nonsense.

He parked the Cadillac a block away from Main Street, in front of the familiar high school, and walked rapidly toward his objective. Wayland's two blocks of business establishments were lightless and serene. I see they still roll up the sidewalks, Danny thought. Nothing had changed. A battered red Christmas bell hung over the entrance to the Corner Drugstore, and hard by, the Acme Jewelry Company's name was glazed on the door, encircled by a prefabricated wreath. Through the dark windows of Montgomery's he could see the jumble of flimsy trivia that denoted the holiday season in a general store.

He walked around the corner, down the side of the drugstore and into the alley, keeping close to the wall of the building. His gloved hand groped along the wall, and when it touched the rusty iron ladder he smiled reminiscently. He leaned against the wall in the shadow and lighted a cigarette. In the momentary flare of the match his face was silhouetted—bony, sharp, and pale, with the unaired pallor of the nocturnal wanderer. The quicksilver of his eyes had dulled to opaque pewter. There was a tic in his cheek, and his hand trembled as he extinguished the match. He drew deeply on the cigarette, and when he had smoked it to the very end he ground it out, pulled down the ladder, and swung upward.

The roof of the old-fashioned building was absolutely flat and had a graveled surface. There was a small water tank in one corner and four skylights near the center, which had been installed to provide light and air to the dark stuffy rectangles of the stores below. They were set in a quadrangle, close together. Each was equipped with a chain to pull the largest pane of glass outward to let in air.

He walked around the cluster of skylights in confusion. He had not remembered that there were so many or that they were so close together. To the best of his recollection the skylight of the drugstore had been in the rear, over the prescription department. This indicated that the forward skylight, nearest the street, must service the Acme Jewelry Store, while the other two probably belonged to the larger quarters of the Montgomery Dry Goods Company. He was annoyed at this failure of his memory and paced sulkily around the humps of glass, peering down into the darkness without being able to see anything. As he reconstructed the interior of the drugstore in his mind he convinced himself that his first impulse had been correct.

The eerie feeling, which had not left him since he drove into Wayland, was beginning to get on his nerves, and he wanted to be done with the whole thing. He walked quickly to the Main Street side of the roof, jerked the chain on the forward skylight, and the pane of glass swung out with a thin complaint. He shouldered his way through the opening, clinging to the steel framework of the skylight, and groped with his dangling feet for the top of a counter. When his feet touched solid surface he distributed his weight on them, let go the framework, and felt in his overcoat pocket for his electric torch.

Before he flashed his light, he knew he had made a mistake. A dark-brown odor, mixture of drugs and face powder, chocolate syrup and ancient dust, found his nostrils. There was no denying it, and he experienced for the moment that wild tug of fear that had accompanied his unconventional entrance into Doc Clancy's place of business twenty years before. He began to sweat as he passed the dim light furtively over the wall cases of ranked merchandise, the dusty sundries, the tired tinsel and artificial poinsettias, the old brown-and-cream onyx soda fountain with the discolored, mirror-backed bar, which bore the legend: "Jumbo soda—15¢" written in soap. He was standing on top of the perfume counter.

Rage shook him that he could have stumbled, from sentiment or stupidity, into such an unprofessional error. He uttered a few unprintable words as he got down and moved to the rear of the store to let himself out the back door. When he came abreast of the prescription room he observed that it also had a skylight, and this improved his humor. He noticed, too, that Doc Clancy's old black safe was still standing in its time-honored place beside the prescription counter. He thought he might as well take what it had in it, as long as he was already there. Not that he expected more than chicken feed.

He sat down on the floor and twirled the knobs of the squat old strongbox experimentally, and in a few seconds the door opened outward. He thrust his hand inside and drew out a packet of papers held together by a rubber band. In the narrow beam of the torch he began to examine them. They were all in the name of Fletcher Bassett.

So much for the captain of industry. He owned the Corner Drugstore in Wayland, Missouri. Or at least he owned it for the time being. With the fascination that attends the rifling of another human being's most intimate papers Danny studied the little bunch of documents in his hand. Aside from the deed to the store, assigned by Harmon Clancy's heirs, they were mostly demands from creditors, notes owed, and a mortgage on the building, along with a ledger of uncollected accounts. Fletcher's bankbook showed a balance of $86.43, and in an envelope affixed to this, the day's receipts reposed. They toted up to $18.99. There were two or three more sheets of frantic figuring and the first draft of a rather pathetic letter, requesting an extension on the current note.

Together with the dismal record of small business there was another page of hen tracks and doodles, attesting to the fact that Fletcher, no matter what his situation, still followed the grail. On this sheet he had estimated the cost of a new soda fountain, a linoleum floor covering, a remodeled store front, and a neon sign. Fletcher had drawn a diagram of this sign for himself with BASSETT in large letters and a mortar-and-pestle symbol. These hallucinations were obviously the products of lonely night watches in the prescription room, when Fletcher could no longer face the reality of what he already owed.

The emotion of pity, long a stranger to Daniel Morgan, stirred in his cool blood. He brooded briefly on the things that can waylay man's aspiration and reduce his dreams to dust and how both ends of a road can lead to bankruptcy, how you can come full circle in your life and find only the bits and pieces of what you had in mind. He mourned for Fletcher, bound and hog-tied, and for himself, fugitive and lost.

When he came to the sealed envelope marked *Personal* in Fletcher's unformed hand, he actually had qualms about opening it, so righteous had he become, but curiosity overcame his newborn ethics. It contained the usual assortment—insurance policy for five thousand dollars, with Mary Kidd Bassett named as beneficiary. That stringy-haired little Kidd girl, Daniel thought. Why, she was just a baby! There were birth certificates of two children, a boy and a girl, and Fletcher's will. At the bottom of the envelope, folded into a sheet of plain paper, was an old yellowed newspaper clipping.

Danny took it out and unfolded it carefully. It bore the blurred photograph of a young woman in a dated wedding dress under a headline that ran:

TWO PROMIMENT FAMILIES UNITED. The marriage of Miss Kathleen Esther Fane to Arthur Pope Patterson, Jr., was solemnized . . .

Danny read, and then worked his way through a flamboyant description of what must have been the greatest social event in Wayland's history.

Well, he had got her—old Stuffed-Shirt Arthur. Arthur the Ass, they had called him. Danny had lost her, and Fletcher had lost her too.

Danny folded the papers neatly and began to restore them to the safe. He weighed the cash receipts of Christmas Eve in Bassett's Corner Drugstore in his hand and decided against them. As he picked up the duns and mortgages and the affecting figures Fletcher had scribbled down without hope, he shook his head. He frowned and rubbed the muscle jumping in his cheek and whistled softly through his teeth, as if he were trying very hard to make up his mind about something.

Suddenly he stood up, withdrew the rich alligator wallet from the inside pocket of his coat, and took out the five thousand dollars in earnest money that Julius had wagered on him. He folded the bills into Fletcher's inventory of improvements, snapped the rubber band around them, and put them back in the safe. He took out a fine linen handkerchief and methodically wiped the fingerprints from the door of the safe from habit and closed it softly.

"Regular damn Robin Hood!" Daniel said to himself, and stretched. He walked out of the back room into the main store, put his foot on a fountain chair, mounted the perfume case, and heaved himself through the skylight, as he had done so many years before.

He emerged on the flat gravel surface of the roof and oriented himself. By trial and error he had eliminated the first two skylights. The other two must belong to the Acme Jewelry Store. How wrong can you be? He had a wavering instinct to flee, but if he expected to make expenses on his troublesome journey into history, he would have to collect the rest of Julius' offer.

He eased over to the third aperture and jerked the chain to pull the window outward and stopped. Her skin had been as white as milk. Her hair curling about the nape of her neck had been a flawless thing. Hers had been a throat fit to bear the necklace of an empress. Diamonds would become her. If she had to abide Arthur, the least she deserved was this. He came to a momentous decision: Angie would have to be disappointed.

He let the chain drop, and the glass swung in with a delicate clangor, like a wind chime. Inside the Acme Jewelry Store a beam of light materialized. Wild apprehension, even terror, rushed over him as his mind grasped the ambush that had been waiting there for him all the time. His throat went dry. He drew his gun and fell back to the edge of the roof, groping with one hand for the top of the ladder.

"Who's there?" the voice demanded, and the glass rattled as it was attacked from inside.

At the edge of the roof he recovered from panic. Borne up by an odd sensation of invincibility, he settled his padded shoulders, drew on his gray suede gloves, and straightened his black homburg. Over his sardonic face a grin flickered, and out of his old arrogant aplomb he made his statement.

"It's me," he said. "Santy Claus!"

The gun cracked and shattered the skylight. He ducked from instinct and hurtled down the ladder. Flattening himself against the soiled walls of the old building, he sidled out of the alley and broke for cover in the pale, waning moonlight.

Before he reached the car he heard the whine of the alarm, and the first running figures converged on the jewelry store.

"Donder and Blitzen!" said Danny. "Get me the hell out of here!"

Around noon the next day an Ohio state trooper on his routine rounds pulled into a filling station for refueling.

"What's new, Pop?" he asked the old man who was pumping gasoline into the motorcycle's tank.

"Nothing much," said the old man. "There was a right curious fellow through here a while ago."

"Yeah?" said the trooper.

"Yeah. Said he was headed for the North Pole."

"You don't say," grinned the trooper. "Did he have whiskers?"

"Nope. Clean-shaved. Didn't look too good either—kind of skinny and sallow. He was real dressy, though. Had a big, new car."

"I guess he was pulling your leg, Pop."

"I dunno. He sounded like he meant what he said."

"Well, there's no accounting for the things people will do," the trooper opined with a yawn, and, putting his foot on the throttle, he went peacefully home to his turkey and mince pie.

Small World

From time immemorial the legends have insisted that there is a sort of magic in the Christmas season—that evil and misery, small or great, are then capable of being put to rights, "so gracious and so hallowed is the time." Over the scars and depredations of the weary earth falls the silent, secret snow; hearts soften and eyes see with a new perspective; men revert to the simple values and the pristine truths, long lost in the hurly-burly of their frantic lives. This is the kind of premise in which a hardheaded businessman like G. Putnam Frobisher would have previously taken little stock. The complications of his busy existence would have given him no time, actually, to examine the merits of the case, but Mr. Frobisher, who was rushing down a shining track somewhat like a locomotive out of control, was brought up short by a curious blocking system which he could not have invented.

If Mr. Frobisher wasn't the busiest executive in the entire world, he was runner-up. He occupied the exact nerve center of the Ajax Corporation, whose vast holdings fanned out in ever-increasing circles, combining institutions of research, mining, manufacturing, distribution, merchandising, communication, financing, subsidiaries, and holding companies into one enormous web whose strands encompassed the earth. In a rare moment of self-examination he had once encountered in his mind an image of himself in the role of a middle-aged spider, sitting there at his ten-foot desk, spinning the Ajax network out of his own vitals. Mr. Frobisher put such thoughts immediately from him. He did not have time for a nervous breakdown.

Frobisher did not look much like a spider. He was a man of powerful build, tall and large-boned, with a long head thatched in gun-metal wire. His face was craggy and intense, with outcroppings of mulishness along the range of his jaw, an imperious nose, and eyes like the business end of a pair of steel drills. He had the face and figure for leadership, along with the other requisites, and he was commonly known to accept no nonsense from his subordinates. Since he had no superiors, if you except God, Frobisher's slightest wish was law, at least in the confines of the Ajax Corporation. He boasted that he never asked anybody to do anything he couldn't do himself, and this was a fact. He had started his career as a tooldresser on an Ajax wildcat, and he knew a man can do anything he takes it into his head to do.

But it had been some time since Frobisher had been bothered with the details. He normally sat at his great desk in his superb office and pushed buttons. Frobisher's button box looked like the battery of a train dispatcher in Grand Central Terminal. In addition to the conventional primary colors, he had buttons in mauve, chartreuse, cerise, and other mutations of the spectrum, so there would be enough colors to go around. He had pushed a button that set off the first charge of dynamite in the excavation for a dam in Asia Minor and a button that swung the last girder into place in a bridge over a wild canyon in Tibet. When Frobisher pushed a button something always happened. It said so on the cover of *Time*.

Knowledgeable people who commented on his rise to power and affluence pointed out that it had been meteoric—a tribute to the system of free enterprise—but Frobisher, first cousin to Atlas at forty-five, was known in some quarters (where the significance of his first initial had been ferreted out) as Gideon, the Ghoul.

He did not know this, any more than he knew that twenty-five years of sweat and slugging had taken a terrific toll on him. A man does not get to be president of practically everything and chairman of the board of everything else without sacrificing a good deal of what is commonly supposed to matter most. So with Frobisher. His business relations were peerless, but his human relations had deteriorated to such an extent that there was no guarantee that he had any. He was surrounded by great galaxies of people but gave his trust to no one, was skeptical of any proffered warmth since he might have to pay off in coin embarrassing to Ajax, and out of sheer preoccupation sometimes could not remember which of their various establishments his wife was occupying at the moment.

This was particularly unfortunate, for Catherine Frobisher was a sweet, sensible woman who had fallen in love with Gideon as a schoolgirl and had never been able to change her mind. From the age of eighteen her principal concern in life had been to please him and make herself useful, so she had become the handmaiden of his ambition, a timid satellite in the wake of a fiery star. She was a farm girl whose natural dairymaid proportions had been honed down by the most rigorous abstention and painstaking effort to the classic mold, just as her native reticence had been abandoned for the extrovert conquest of culture and society. She marched shoulder to shoulder with her mate, whenever she could get close enough to him.

The fact that Catherine was mistress of apartments and houses in New York, Westchester,

Palm Beach, Palm Springs, Acapulco, London, and Nice depressed rather than elated her. She had a housewifely soul and worried about whether the linen had been aired and the silver polished and counted in some establishment she hadn't been to lately. When she thought of home, she never thought of any of these places but of a four-room house in Claremore, Oklahoma, she had presided over as a bride, where Gid came home every night and kissed her on the mouth.

Their only child had been born there, and it seemed to Catherine that they had never been quite so happy since they left this humble cot for the half-timbered, pseudo-Tudor mansion in Tulsa, which presaged their rise in the world. Kay had disappointed her father, whose businesslike determination to lavish on her all the things he had never had himself resulted in fiasco. Two years before, she had defied him by contracting an alleged mésalliance with a football player, and in an incredible scene he had instructed her never to darken his door again and cut her off with a dollar.

Catherine, whose divided loyalties had then chafed her neck like an iron collar, had stood helplessly by, torn with pity for the four of them and with fear for the future stretching her apart.

"Gid, Gid," she had pleaded. "Can't you remember when we were young?"

"I can't remember when I was a damn fool," Gideon said tersely. People were people, he asseverated, and had to be dealt with according to the established rules of personnel. It was her first inkling that he had finally got too busy. It is one thing to be busy, powerful, and effective. It is quite another to be too busy, for when power corrupts it ceases to be effective. A cold draft, like the wind off an iceberg, blew across her heart.

"He seems a decent boy, if you could only get to know him, Gid," she had pursued.

"There is no reason why I *should* get to know him," Gid declared unreasonably, quivering with betrayed trust from the quarter he had least expected it. "No daughter of mine would sneak out in the night to go off with that insulting clown! Ergo, I have no daughter!"

"Kay would say you were making like King Lear," Catherine said.

"Don't mention her name to me!" he shouted, the cords standing out in his forehead. "She has made fools of us and yet you take her part!"

Catherine's persistent optimism had suffered a death blow on this occasion, and she felt doubly deprived. Kay had flown, and Kay's father had turned into a raucous stranger. She could not reach him, and in the midst of her wearying pursuit of social good works and house and apartment management she had thoughtful spells of wondering why she did any and everything she did. There did not seem to be much sense in it any more. A melancholy shadow came to rest in her brown eyes, and her damask cheek paled.

Sometimes she had fitful dreams that depicted Gideon going down to destruction. But he showed no sign of relenting, and Kay was a chip off her father's granite. She could no more capitulate than he could.

As the months multiplied, Gideon, whose wounds were deeper than he cared to admit, flung himself into his business with increasing fervor. The war had given new impetus to Ajax's great projects, and he was flying between New York and Washington, flying to Downing Street and Paris for weekend conferences, hurtling to South America for twenty-four-hour stays, and manipulating the complex strands of his enterprise like some gigantic weaver. All else had become secondary.

To further some of his important transactions with the administration in Washington, Gideon had stooped. He had begun to send orchids and bracelets and otherwise to curry favor with a lady of government influence in the capital, and he found himself spending considerable time in a house in Alexandria, Virginia. Gideon had rarely lent himself to such conniving, but new situations create new methods, and he was one of those people who have come to accept the notion that the end justifies the means.

It had better be said that the means struck him as more or less irksome. Gideon loved his wife, when he could get a moment to give to the matter, and he had never given much thought to other

women. He was somewhat dismayed at the disposition of his new friend to take his attentions
more seriously than he had intended them, but his
original purpose remained strong. The situation
had inevitably come to the attention of a
Washington columnist, who seized on it with
gusto. Gideon brushed off the slimy implication
and chose to operate on the theory that Catherine
did not read such trash and was too sane to take
stock in idle gossip. He hadn't seen much of her
lately, but he didn't presume that her character
had changed.

But one morning late in December he had
come down to breakfast to find the table laid for
one. He observed this phenomenon with a twinge
of surprise, for whenever he was in residence his
wife's pleasure was so immense that she arose at
the crack of dawn, sat beaming at the table, creat-
ing his toast and pouring out his coffee with her
own hands.

"Isn't Mrs. Frobisher feeling well?" he asked
the maid who brought in his eggs.

"Mrs. Frobisher isn't here, sir," the girl said.

"Well, where is she?" Gideon asked testily.

"I don't know, sir," the girl answered with a
start. "She left yesterday."

"Didn't she say where she was going?"

"No, sir."

It seemed to Gideon that it was rather mean of
Catherine to go off to Palm Beach without telling
him. He had been thinking of getting down there

himself. He was very tired. They might have gone together.

As he was being driven toward the Ajax Tower in mid-town Manhattan, he noticed for the first time that it seemed to be Christmas. The gutters were crusted with gray ice, and the bitter wind flapped the jaded greens and garlands on the store fronts of New York. The streets were packed with tatterdemalion crowds wrestling unwieldly bundles, and the red-nosed Santa Clauses stood over their mangy iron pots covered with chicken wire, dingling their little bells for the poor. Gideon regarded the holiday scene bleakly. Except for its obvious bearing on the economic setup of the nation, it all seemed to him to be a patent waste of time.

He was, at this point, oppressed by a sudden recollection of Catherine and himself shopping for a doll in the variety store at Claremore, Oklahoma, the year Kay was four. He remembered that they had bought the $2.98 doll, though they hardly had the wherewithal to eat. But she had been such a sweet, eager little girl. There hadn't been a doll in Claremore good enough for her. Her father had promised himself to buy her a Paris doll someday. He had delivered, but to what purpose?

Gideon rode up in his special elevator to the top of the tower, where he was obsequiously greeted by the minions who danced attendance on him, but he continued to be unsettled by his brief excursion into the past. As his vast problems claimed him, the wraith of Kay's ecstatic crooning to the $2.98 doll buzzed in his ear like a gnat and shattered his concentration. She had always been the apple of his eye, and it was for this reason that he could not forgive her.

Gideon pushed the purple button and Miss Belton came into the office. "Please put in a call to Mrs. Frobisher at the Palm Beach house," he directed, and sat back to wait. For some reason he badly wanted the reassurance of Catherine's voice.

When the buzzer sounded, Gideon seized the receiver and said "Hello!" with unusual warmth.

"Mrs. Frobisher isn't there," Miss Belton reported.

"You mean she's out?"

"The caretaker says the house is closed," said Miss Belton.

"Oh," Gideon said, chagrined before his executive secretary. "Well, never mind."

Now where had she got to when he needed her? Gideon mused with annoyance, and dialed the house at Rye on his private wire.

"Let me speak to Mrs. Frobisher, Baker," he said.

"Mrs. Frobisher isn't here, sir."

Gideon wondered whether you could ask a circumspect butler when he had last seen your wife. He became crafty. "When she was there yesterday did she say where she was going?"

"It was the day before yesterday," Baker said. "Mrs. Baker helped her pack. But I don't think she mentioned her destination, sir."

A light beading of perspiration broke out on Gideon's forehead.

"Thank you, Baker," he said.

"Merry Christmas, Mr. Frobisher," Baker said kindly, and to his disgust Gideon swallowed too hard for comfort. He had the appalling feeling that he might be about to cry.

"Same to you, Baker."

"Mrs. Baker and I would like to thank you for the gift," Baker said.

"Oh, that," Gideon dissembled. Such matters were handled by his business management, and he had no idea what it was. He had the grace to feel slightly ashamed.

The rest of the day Ajax's great projects suffered while Gideon and his immediate office staff endeavored to complete phone calls to Palm Springs, London, Paris, Nice, Rome, and Mexico. By four o'clock no trace of Mrs. Frobisher had been found, and Miss Belton had systematically begun to check all airlines, steamship companies, railroads, and other means of transportation, but to no avail.

Gideon had begun to wear a track in the carpet of his office from his restless pacing. When the bell of his private telephone wire jangled at 5 P.M. he seized on it with relief.

"Alexandria, Virginia, is calling," the operator

intoned.

Gideon swore. He cursed his own folly for ever having parted with his private number. He had had every intention of confining his Washington peccadilloes to the vicinity of Washington. He had known that the lady in question was as bold as brass. He must have been mad.

"He's out of town," Gideon hissed into the mouthpiece, and hung up.

He buzzed Miss Belton and instructed her that the office was to accept no telephone calls from Alexandria, Virginia, for any reason. This was an exigency with which he could not cope in the present crisis.

He ordered his car, shrugged himself into his overcoat, and hurried downstairs before the telephone could ring again. As he waited on the curb for Jefferson the home-going crowds skirled past him, heads bent against the cold wind, chattering with each other like so many monkeys, Gideon thought with irritation. The mechanical chimes of a department store began to play a mechanical carol, and a woman dragging a small girl by the hand stopped to listen and stepped on his feet. As she lifted the child in her arms, Gideon suddenly felt unbearably solitary.

He drove up the Avenue to his opulent house, entertaining himself with the fantasy that Catherine would be sitting there in the fifty-foot drawing room when he arrived.

She wasn't.

A strange woman answered his ring. He presumed she was the housekeeper, but he couldn't remember.

"Good evening, Mr. Frobisher," the woman said with a look of embarrassment.

The house seemed empty and dead.

"Where is everybody?" Gid asked.

"I let the girls off for church. We didn't expect you for dinner, sir."

"What day is it?" Gid asked.

"Thursday, the twenty-second," the woman said with surprise. "They were having some Christmas music . . ."

"It's all right," he said wearily. "I'm not hungry."

The telephone jangled and she went to answer it. "Alexandria, Virginia, is calling, sir," she reported.

He groaned. "I'm out," he shouted. "Tell her I'm out and I won't be back!"

He then instructed her to accept no calls from Virginia. He was outraged. The effrontery of that woman, intruding on a man in the privacy of his home! He couldn't think why she had ever seemed even vaguely attractive to him. Well, the bill would soon be out of the committee, and it would no longer be necessary to play the role. Gid climbed his vaulted stair, clicked off the telephones, and went supperless to bed, where he passed a sleepless night.

In the pearly morning light he felt and looked

haggard. But the very act of shaving and putting on his expensive shoes and fine linen and good clothes restored his confidence, and he said to himself that the guiding spirit of one of the world's largest corporations would not be stumped by the peccadilloes of women. The minute he got to the office he proposed to locate Mrs. Frobisher and give her a good talking to— call her on the carpet, the way one did erring people. By the time he arrived at presumed sanctuary, having ascertained that Catherine had not surreptitiously reappeared in the night, he had worked himself into a wholesome fury.

Fuel to this fire was the obvious disorganization of his ordinarily impeccable staff. They were all rushing about, exchanging gaudy packages and the greetings of the season. The fluty laughter of the girls, paper cups of some sort of nauseating punch, and sticky dishes of candy had turned the place into a shambles and attested to the fact that they had not expected him. His taut arrival dropped a pall over the Christmas merrymaking, and with the scuffle and bustle of children caught in misdemeanor, they began to get back to their desks. This incensed him, for nothing could now please him, and since they chose to feel that he was not a human being, he proposed to live up to their judgment.

Gideon threw down his attaché case and started to punch one button after another. The board began to resemble a Fourth of July spectacle. One frightened face after another appeared in the door, and since Gideon could not bring himself to say: "I have lost my wife and you have to find her," and he had to say something, he took occasion to criticize and revile everything they had all done for the past twelve months and reduced them, one after another, to terror or tears. The wind of his humor blew through the building like a hurricane, and people cowered before it.

When he had subdued everybody within reach, including four vice-presidents, Gideon shut his door and locked it, sat down at his desk, and put his head in his hands. He had made no progress with the main event. He looked venomously at his throbbing box of buttons and saw them for what they were—useless. He could push them until kingdom come and they would not restore Catherine to him. How could the president of Ajax push a button and tell his vassal on the other end to call the police, the hospitals, the Bureau of Missing Persons and announce that Mrs. G. Putnam Frobisher had disappeared? It was unthinkable. Face must be saved by some means not at this moment clear to him. The tragedy was that no one of these lines led to a person in whom he could confide—certainly not now, after the morning's depredations. Gideon had an impulse to tear his vaunted push-button system out by the roots and throw it out the window.

But he was no nearer to the solution. He had to do something. Suppose she were ill or hurt, struck down, an unidentified woman with brown eyes and a soft cloud of dark hair, wearing a wistful expression . . . Or my wife Catherine, having left my bed and board . . . Not that, surely not that.

The telephone rang. Gideon's trembling hand closed over the receiver.

"On your call to Alexandria. . . ."

Gideon moaned and set the instrument back in the cradle without speaking.

Now if Kay were here, she could tell him what to do. She was a bright little thing—mind like a steel trap. Took after her old man, people said. He let himself consider that flyaway creature, hazel-eyed, fawn-like, who had been his daughter once. She was the only person who had ever beaten him. He had not let himself think how much he missed her, but his weakness for her engulfed him in a tide of misery. What had possessed him to cut himself free of the dearest thing in life?

"Kay, Kay, where are you?" he asked the silence.

As if in response, his private wire jangled maddeningly.

"On your call——"

"I have no call," Gideon bellowed. "Kindly do not annoy me again!"

But with that well-known persistence of the long-distance system, it kept up at intervals throughout the afternoon and eventually drove him out of the office.

Christmas shopping had reached a climax and

was sloping off. Gideon, having forgotten to summon his car, walked aimlessly down the darkling street toward Radio City, where the gaping crowds stood about admiring the blue Norwegian spruce hung with a thousand beautiful baubles. He stared at it, and its beauty moved him strangely. Then it occurred to him how desultory is such pleasure when unshared. It had been years since Gideon had thought he had time for a stroll around the streets of New York, but now it occurred to him that he did not seem to have anything to do, when everybody else had so much, and also he did not have anybody to do it with.

He tried to think of a friend he could call on the spur of the moment and say, "Come on and have a spot of dinner with me and we'll take a walk and I'll tell you my troubles!" He couldn't think of anybody. It did not seem reasonable that a man in his position did not have at least one friend, but nobody came to mind. Except Catherine, of course. This was the sort of thing she loved—ducking into some little French hole-in-the-wall and having some outrageous thing like snails or mussels, and window-shopping—hanging onto his arm, smiling up into his eyes, talking things out. They had done that when they first came to New York and were young and bedazzled. Catherine was the one he wanted—but he seemed to have mislaid her.

He began to feel sorry for himself. Alone, at Christmas! How could they do this to him? As he

passed St. Patrick's he felt as unloved as the Little
Match Girl. A dismal Santa Claus was standing at
the corner of Fiftieth Street, huddling over his pot.

"How's business?" Gideon asked, largely to
hear the sound of his own voice.

"Terrible!" said Santa Claus. "They don't think
of nobody but themselves."

Gideon opened up his alligator wallet and withdrew a hundred-dollar bill.

"It is a common habit," he said bitterly.

The man's eyes glazed and Gideon was startled
himself, but he felt slightly better.

He walked on for a few blocks and then went
home, where Mrs. Carrick (he had discovered that
was her name) told him that Alexandria, Virginia,
was still calling.

"I told you I am not taking calls," he
announced in a dying voice, for the fight had gone
out of him. "Good night!" He climbed the stairs
wearily and took a sleeping pill.

He did not sleep. As he tossed and turned he
decided that this had gone on long enough. Something had certainly happened to Catherine.
Perhaps she had been run down, mugged, kid-
napped, suffered amnesia from shock. He must do
something. His anxiety overwhelmed him, and he
got up and paced the floor of the bedroom and the
dressing room and eventually the library, drawing
room, pantry, and corridors, prowling like a lost
dog. He could scarcely wait for dawn to get down
to the office and do something about it.

Pale and trembling and at the breaking point from worry, he bolted out of the house at 9 A.M. and sped to the office. The streets were deserted and he wondered why his building was dark and silent, and there was only one elevator in operation.

"What in the name of heaven has happened?" Gideon demanded of the old man in his shirt sleeves who was reading the paper. "Where is everybody?"

"It's Saturday," the old man said. "Christmas Eve. Everybody is home who's got a home."

"Oh yes," said Gideon, wincing, and asked to be taken up. He sat down in the office and wondered what to do. Inspiration deserted him. He fiddled with papers on his desk. He tried to concentrate on the pressing problems of industry. At last he had time and he couldn't think. Catherine's face bloomed between his eyes and whatever they looked on. Kay's angry little countenance, subconscious souvenir of their final meeting, stormed up at him from the confusion of his papers. As he strove to put his mind on the astronomical figures before him, it was borne in on Gideon that he wanted nothing else in life but his wife and daughter. With a great burst of energy he began to shuffle through his private files, trying to locate the address of Kay's first habitation after her marriage. He remembered having put it somewhere in a fit of rage. He wrecked the neat filing system, but he could not find it. When he had completed his depredations he got up and stalked out with an unformed idea of checking police stations and hospitals himself. The snow was falling in wet blobs, and the city seemed deserted.

The peregrinations of Gideon on that fateful Christmas Eve are almost too depressing to be described. All the avenues he pursued turned into dead-end streets. No hospital had admitted Catherine. No police blotter bore evidence of an accident or a violent event that might have included a brown-eyed woman whose name he could hardly bring himself to mention. As his fruitless search progressed, Gideon began to make bargains with the absent Catherine, with disinherited Kay, with his miserable self, with God. Eventually he relinquished all but the latter.

"Let them be safe," he prayed incoherently. "And everything will be different from now on." He accompanied this with mental pictures of himself writing out fat checks for almost everybody in need, before it occurred to him that the gift without the giver is bare. He then revised his entire philosophy of life and established for the future a completely new set of principles in all his operations. This included hundred-percent bonuses for everybody he had wounded in the office the day before.

As darkness fell he stumbled toward the house on Fifth Avenue because he did not know where else to go. The snow had ceased, and the night was blue and brittle, stricken with starshine, and clear as a crystal bell. Gideon was not aware of it. He examined the world through a mist of tears.

Somebody had put a holly wreath on the bronze door of his house, but it only made him think of a funeral.

Mrs. Carrick admitted the appalling apparition of the former tycoon, gave him a surprised glance and a cheerful Merry Christmas.

"Merry Christmas," Gideon echoed in the hollow voice of doom.

"Mrs. Frobisher is in the library," Mrs. Carrick said in a routine way.

"What!" Gideon shouted, and almost knocked the woman down to gain the stairs, which he mounted three at a time.

She was standing at the fireplace, winding a swag of holly around the candelabra. The candlelight fell on her face, and she was smiling to herself. She had on a long rustling taffeta gown in that shade of bronze which complemented her hair, and her eyes were shining. He had never seen anything so beautiful, and he shut his tired eyes against her radiant presence for fear it was a hallucination. The relief that washed over him was so intense that he almost stumbled and fell. He said later that he didn't know whether to kiss her or kill her.

"Catherine," he croaked. "Where have you been?"

"Gid!" she said. "Darling!"

They came together in an embrace that almost

stifled them both.

"Giddy," she said, using that horrible nickname that he had always despised but which now sounded rather wonderful. "I was so worried."

"*You* were worried!" he roared.

"I couldn't think what had happened to you."

"Me!" he repeated stupidly.

"It really isn't like you to not tell me where you're going."

"But I've been right *here* all the time. You're the one who didn't tell me where you were going. And, by the way, where was it?"

"But, Gid, I tried to tell you. Anyway, we're both here now, so what difference does it make?"

"None," said Gideon firmly. "Kiss me. I've been so busy lately I haven't kissed anybody."

"You certainly have!"

"Have what? Kissed anybody?" he asked, the cold claw of fear at his heart.

"Been busy," she said. "Too busy."

"You didn't answer my question," he said hurriedly. "Where *were* you?"

"Let's sit down," she said. "You look tired, sweetie."

"Tired!" Gideon shouted. "I'm *exhausted*. I've been hunting you for three days! I'm about to drop dead."

"Maybe you ought to lie down," she said, "before you do." She sat on the sofa and took his head in her silken lap.

The peace which this gesture engendered in

him struck him as so delicious that he could not bear to break the silence and made no resistance when she massaged his temples and kissed him on his nose. He sighed profoundly and caught her hand and brought it to his lips.

"Gid," she said, staring down intently at the subdued gladiator. "I have something to tell you."

"Well, what is it?" he asked drowsily. "Tell me."

"Promise me you won't explode."

He sat up with a jolt. "What is it?" he asked tensely. "Don't keep me in suspense. I simply can't take anything else. You don't know what I've been through."

"You're getting too old for it, too," said Catherine. "You're a grandfather."

His jaw dropped.

"It's a boy," she said.

"My God," said Gideon, feeling his skull prickle. "When—well, how is she? Where's that good-for-nothing husband of hers?"

"He's in Korea," said Catherine.

"Oh," Gideon said brokenly. "Is she—is my Kay all right?" He felt as if he were going to cry again.

"She's fine. She named the baby for you."

"Well, why did you go off and leave her alone?" he blustered. "Why didn't you let me know? Why aren't we both down there?"

"That's what I mean," Catherine said. "I couldn't imagine what had happened to you. I kept calling and calling. Nobody would say

where you were or give me any information. You
didn't answer your private wires. You never came
home. I was afraid you were sick or in trouble.
I had to come home to find out about *you*. I
was *frantic*."

"Where did you say you were?" Gideon asked,
feeling as if he might faint any minute.

"I didn't say. But I was in Alexandria, Virginia.
Kay's in the Post Hospital there."

Gideon's mind reeled.

"They've been stationed in Washington for
over a year. When he went overseas Kay stayed
on. The baby was due and she didn't have anywhere else to go. I hated to deceive you, Gid, but
I've been to Alexandria several times."

"You have!" Gideon said, his blood running
quite cold.

"Christmas is a time for forgiving," Catherine
said. "For beginning over. Don't you think so?"

"Yes, I do," he mumbled. "I certainly do."

"It would be fun, having a baby in the house,"
Catherine said wistfully.

Gideon's throat relaxed and his chest
expanded. "Well, of course," he said belligerently
"Where else would the baby be? You don't suppose I'd permit a daughter of mine to go racket-
ing around the country alone with a baby!"

"I love you," Catherine said passionately.
"You're impossible, but I love you anyway.
Merry Christmas, Giddy."

"Merry Christmas, dear," he said abstractedly.

"How soon can you get your things together, Catherine? I'm in a hurry."

She observed that he had already reverted to type, but it didn't seem to matter.

A couple of hours later, as the plane drifted down over the crystalline domes of wintry Washington, she sighed luxuriously and said, "How small the world is," and while Gideon searched her face for ambiguity she added, "And isn't it lucky, or we wouldn't be here tonight."

He agreed fervently, and that was the last time the subject ever came up even obliquely. But when Gideon gets too busy these days or starts thinking of himself as a colossus he remembers last Christmas. Knowing how small the world can be and also how enormous, Gideon finds it impossible to be anything but humbly grateful, awash with peace and absolutely overflowing with good will for men, women, and children.

Santa Claus
and the
Tenth Avenue
Kid

It was the last year of the war, and the raw material for the manufacture of department-store Santa
Clauses was at its lowest ebb—a critical shortage.
The old men already had jobs. They had come out
of retirement, real and enforced, a Pickwickian
crew, to take over the management of elevators,
store counters, and accounting ledgers. They had
become waiters, bus boys, and bellhops, painters,
carpenters, and plumbers, sharpening up their old
skills and beginning life over. They had become
doormen with rigid backs and white cotton
gloves. They were practicing law and medicine
again. Advertisements in the paper read, wonder

of wonders: "Nobody under 45 need apply. Position permanent." It was the year of old men, but it left quite a hole in the department-store Santa Claus market.

This was certainly the only reason Mr. Sears ever fell heir to the red velvet breeches and ermine-trimmed tunic, the knee-high, shiny black boots, and the luxuriant, silver, real-hair wig and beard that belonged to the department store of Sampson & Cole. Though Mr. Sears was temperamentally not suited to the role of Santa Claus, he looked quite convincing in the part, owing to the fact that he had a nose like a cherry, and a round belly, which shook, whether he laughed or not, like a bowlful of jelly. These physical characteristics derived from a lifetime devoted to a career of alcoholism and other vices too numerous to mention. The only drawback to the whole thing was his glacial blue eyes, in which there was no semblance of a twinkle. But the haggard personnel manager of Sampson & Cole, faced with a Santa Claus-less sixth floor in December, saw fit to overlook this.

Mr. Sears had no taste for the job. His interest in any job, unless you count what he might have referred to as a second-story stint, was nil. Sampson & Cole's rather panic-stricken advertisement for a Santa Claus was forcibly pointed out to Mr. Sears by his parole officer and a social service worker in the Municipal Rehabilitation Shelter, where Mr. Sears was spending a customary three weeks allotted to him for reorientation by the state. Mr. Sears' previous address had been the State Prison Farm, where he had sojourned five years, paying off a slight debt to society. It seemed that he had maneuvered a widow out of her life savings.

This term, however, was only one of many. Mr. Sears' record was as long as a country road and just as bumpy. It extended over a period of roughly forty years and was rife with petty larceny, grand larceny, robbery, and confidence matters. At the age of ten Mr. Sears had swiped from a hardware store a pair of skates and had run afoul of the Juvenile Court. At sixteen he had made off with a new motorcycle while hiring out as a delivery boy for a drugstore. He had wound up in the reformatory for eighteen months, from which he emerged with a lot of new ideas and a nickname that followed him the rest of his life. He was Stretch Sears from then on, and at twenty-one Stretch Sears was arrested for having stolen an automobile. He always had had a mechanical turn of mind. He had progressed easily to safecracking, which was quite popular in his youth.

Mr. Sears was not a particularly engaging personality. He was by now a rather dour old man with perennial dyspepsia from intermittent years of prison food and, in the intervals, long bouts with cheap whiskey and the hunted, haunted life of the ex-convict. He had no great regard for people, except as grist for the mill of his peculiar talents. In short, he was not the happy, wistful bum toward whom the careless heart of a passer-by is wont to yearn.

Still, the people who came in contact with Mr. Sears in the soberer interludes of his career continued to feel that there was something in him— that he was reclaimable—though the facts were against them. This probably was the reason he had been able to charm the widow out of her three thousand dollars. But even more perspicacious people, like Judge Chambers, the parole officer, and the case-hardened social worker, Miss Webster, clung to that quality in Mr. Sears which seemed to intimate that it is never too late to start over.

"Of course, it's only temporary," Judge Chambers said, discussing the Sampson & Cole job with his charge. "Just three or four weeks' work. But that'll get you on your feet. Give you an opportunity to look around. It's a great time, you know, for fellows your age. After Christmas we'll certainly be able to line you up something permanent. Some nice, light job that'll pay you a living."

Mr. Sears pondered that he probably could pick up a nice light-fingered job in the Christmas crowd.

"I really believe you'll enjoy it," Miss Webster urged, her plain, earnest face warming with the thought that if Mr. Sears could ever once be surrounded by the sweet innocence of childhood, the dear, trusting, upturned faces, the hot little hands in his, regeneration would set in immediately. "It will give you confidence." Miss Webster colored slightly at this ill-chosen word.

Mr. Sears felt his acid stomach turning, but he reasoned that it would be one way to get rid of the watchdogs of the Municipal Rehabilitation Shelter and back into circulation. It was almost too much to bear thinking about—cavorting around in false whiskers and a red monkey suit— but Mr. Sears was tired. Sometimes it seemed to him that an honest dollar might be fairly interesting for a change. He was getting too old to run. Most of his friends were behind bars or dead; and on occasion, such as now, he felt too exhausted to battle organized society and thought there might be some point in putting himself in Judge Chambers' hands and turning into a respectable janitor. It was a terrible end, but he was getting so that he had to have his sleep.

"Well," he said, "might give it a whirl."

"It's good pay," Judge Chambers warmed to the subject. "Twenty dollars a week and lunch in the store cafeteria."

Miss Webster accompanied him to Sampson & Cole's, to be on the safe side. She said she didn't want him to get lost; but Mr. Sears knew that she didn't want him to change his mind and thereby sink into the gutter of his old life. Mr. Shaw, the personnel manager, gave him one look, observed that he had the figure and the beak for the job, was faintly chilled by the arctic blue of his eyes, and told him to report to the alteration room of the men's clothing department to have the red suit fitted.

Three hours later, Stretch Sears had been metamorphosed into Santa Claus.

He had never felt so conspicuous. Santa Claus' office was buried in a white papier-mâché mountain on the sixth floor, sprinkled with tinsel silver dust and banked with boraxed cornflakes. There was a Dutch door to this enchanted place, over which the eager young could peer at Kris Kringle himself, interviewing one of their number on the subject of his personal Christmas wishes. The office was banked with the most expensive and desirable toys in the Sampson & Cole stock, obviously placed there for purposes of promotion. If any youthful pleader should happen to be stumped, through embarrassment or loss of memory, he could just look around and point and say, "That!" Which information Mr. Sears was to note on a small slip of paper and convey to the attention of the child's accompanying relative. It was all very simple.

Santa Claus' office was stacked with fabulous dolls that closed their eyes and came accompanied by wardrobes suitable to every known occasion, including the coronation of a king. It was full of rolling toys and dappled rocking horses with wild glass eyes, big velvet pandas, and whole circuses replete with clowns, equestrienne

dancers in pink ballet skirts, and real steam cal-
liopes. There were great flotillas of miniature
destroyers and warships, ack-ack guns, and
armies of lead soldiers. There were music boxes
and phonographs and singing tops. There were
fire trucks you could sit in and dollhouses with
real electric lights. All the treasures of childhood
were here collected around Santa Claus' enormous red leather armchair. But the *pièce de résistance* of the collection was a magnificent airplane
model of shining, silvery aluminum, exquisite in
detail, equipped with batteries of lights, red and
blue, with landing gear that could be raised and
lowered, tailpieces that could be angled, pro-
pellers that whirred with the most convincing
sound, and an unbelievably complete instrument
panel. Needless to say, this gadget, which was
almost too wonderful to be considered a toy,
interested even the jaundiced eye of Mr. Sears. He
always had liked mechanical things. The airplane
model was priced at $59.50. It was suspended just
outside Santa Claus' office, and it was the cyno-
sure of all masculine eyes, fathers' and sons'
alike.

It cannot be truthfully said that Mr. Sears was a
charming Santa Claus. He was on the gruff side
(although he honestly tried to live up to his character) and even made one little girl with round
sausage curls and fat legs wail aloud by the mere
rumbling of his voice. When her mother retrieved
her from the chute leading from Santa's office she

glared at Mr. Sears as if he might have pinched her darling; and Mr. Sears looked her up and down with his cold blue eyes, which seemed to make the back of her neck feel chilly. Indeed, several grown people had the inarticulate feeling that he was a strange and vaguely sinister kind of Santa Claus. But they reassured themselves by looking at his benign belly and his cherry nose and did not quite get around to realizing that his eyes were odd.

The first day or two he was tense and nervous. He never had been around children in his life. They bored him, and he often had the impulse to kick some of the spoiled ones where it would do the most good, and the scared, timid ones nonplused him. He did not know what to do to make them feel at ease or to ingratiate himself with them. The extroverts and the curious who clambered on his knee and pulled at his beard unnerved him most of all. He didn't know what to say; he was afraid of making a slip that would get him, and probably Judge Chambers, into trouble. Miss Webster had cautioned him especially about lapsing into profanity and had warned him to keep an even temper, no matter what happened.

At the end of the first day he was exhausted from all this unnatural self-discipline and made plans to skip; but Miss Webster was waiting at the employees' entrance when he emerged all set to hit a saloon, and she convoyed him back to the Municipal Rehabilitation Shelter, asking him bright questions all the way about how it had gone. She seemed to imply that he had had tough sledding; some vestige of pride in Mr. Sears caused him to deny her this satisfaction. He said tartly that it had been okay.

Mr. Sears, who had taken this job only to escape surveillance and make a getaway, soon discovered that he was to be accompanied morning and night to and from the door of Sampson & Cole. This frustration added to his mounting restlessness as the occupant of Santa Claus' office and made him brood on desperate matters. With something approaching hatred he stared at the line of noisy children waiting, never too patiently, for his services. To this was added speculation when he looked at their hovering mothers, mostly wearing expensive fur coats and dangling fine alligator and calfskin handbags, which were no doubt crammed with fresh green currency. The clientele of Sampson & Cole was exclusive and rich. The only thing that restrained him was the customary nightly searching at the exit by the store detective. It seemed to Mr. Sears that it just wouldn't be worth while. His inconvenient memories of prison deterred him; but this, too, made him sad. He felt that he was losing his grip.

After the first few days the tension eased a bit. Mr. Sears got together a speech, which he uttered by rote to each newcomer, and it seemed to satisfy. The children were more interested in what they wanted than they were in him anyway. As he wrote down their unreasonable demands and handed each one the lollipop and the red balloon with "Sampson & Cole" on it in white letters, he disliked them all heartily. They were, in truth and in many ways, creatures of another world, a world that Mr. Sears in his tenderest youth had never inhabited. They were the sheltered children of privilege, some polite and some not, some avaricious, greedy, and pugnacious, some quiet, pleasant, and kind, but all strangers in that deep sense of the word. There could be between them and this weather-beaten old derelict no happy concourse of ideas or emotions. They could come to only superficial terms. But Mr. Sears minded his business and tried hard.

"Come in, sister," he would bellow to a pigtailed mite. "Come into old Santy Claus' office."

The child would advance, timorously or boldly, depending on her nature, and sometimes drop him a curtsy or sometimes manage to kick his shins. Either might throw Mr. Sears off, but he bore up.

"Now, what would the little lady like Santa Claus to leave in her stocking?" he would inquire stickily, affecting a grimace of a grin and leaning closer for the confession.

The little girl would swallow, take a deep breath, and reel off the names of ten or twelve presents.

"But what would you like best of all?" he would urge, and when the decision came he would write it down.

"Just hand this note to your mother," he would instruct, and pass out the lollipop and the red balloon. Sometimes he would forget and say "your maw" or "your old lady," but the children, who were all young, never seemed to notice.

He varied the formula for the boys.

"How-de-do, son!"

"Hello," from the round-eyed child.

"Have you been a good boy?"

They all bobbed their heads in eager acquiescence, although Mr. Sears could tell from looking at them that it was a distinct overstatement. They had all probably been little hellions for at least three hundred days of the year.

"Now tell me, man to man, what you want me to put in your sock."

They always had the answer to that.

Three weeks of this pap would have been stultifying to somebody who had led a less racy existence than Mr. Sears. To him it was almost worse than prison. He fomented in his mind plans for escape, but by night he was too tired and by day he was too busy. As Christmas drew nearer the crowds increased, and the line in front of Santa Claus' office grew longer. The greeting, the questioning, the send-off were repeated until they became like a worn phonograph record, squeaking and repellent. The children's faces blurred into a montage of toothy and snaggle-toothed grins, princess coats, round hats, little gloved hands, and restive feet. Sometimes he thought that if he had to look at another brat he'd throw up. They were all alike, cut from the same rich cloth with the same pair of shears. They hadn't seemed like that when he was young. Well, he reckoned that children changed, got softer with the years, like grown people.

It was the day before Christmas Eve that he got the rude shock. Santa Claus had just called it a day and was ready to shut up shop. He stood up, groaning, and went to the Dutch door to close the upper half. The warning bell sounded, and the crowds were surging toward the elevators and escalators, towing their reluctant young. As he reached for the half door to pull it to, he looked down.

The Tenth Avenue Kid was standing there.

He was a small, pallid boy of indeterminate age. He could have been anywhere from eight to eleven. He had on a pair of dirty denim pants, an old pullover fraying at the edges, and a felt beanie covered with the tops of soft-drink bottles. He was gloveless and overcoatless and grimy. He was so completely out of place in the plush environment of Sampson & Cole that Mr. Sears could not imagine how he had got past all the floorwalkers and salesclerks and managed to look around. It was obvious to Mr. Sears' practiced eye that he had been looking around rather thoroughly.

"Hello, son!" he boomed, getting into his routine almost without thinking that this was no prospect for Sampson & Cole.

"Can it!" said the Tenth Avenue Kid.

For a moment Mr. Sears felt quite happy, as if he had come home; but then he remembered himself. He looked at the unwholesome sprout before him and knew he didn't have to be bothered.

"I reckon you came over to give your instructions to Sandy Claus," Mr. Sears said with heavy sarcasm. "Have you been a good boy this year?"

"Have you?" inquired the Tenth Avenue Kid.

Mr. Sears started in surprise, but he felt a warm tingle of appreciation. "That ain't no part of this here setup," he remarked, speaking naturally for the first time in three weeks.

"Don't give me that stuff," the Tenth Avenue Kid said with the simple wisdom of the hard-bitten. "You ain't real."

"Whadda ya mean, I ain't real? You see me standing here, don'tcha?"

"You're just a man," the Kid said.

Mr. Sears wished, for once, that he could live up to this lofty denomination.

"You can fool babies and dopes," the Kid went on arrogantly (he was obviously not one of the wistful poor). "But I ain't no dope."

Mr. Sears regarded the skinny, taut little figure before him, with its lank lock of black hair hanging between the blazing blue eyes and its proud, intrepid stance, and he felt a twinge of something like rheumatism in his left side. It had been a long time since Mr. Sears had been bothered with affection for any human being—not since Miney

Richards, his old pal, got it in a stick-up. He hardly recognized this emotion, which was more like a physical pain; but anyway, pity stirred in him or some memory of himself when he was small. He had been anti-social for a long time, and he didn't like children; but there was something about this Kid that got next to you.

He pondered this last pronouncement, and then he said, as winningly as he knew how, "Well, take it or leave it, I'm Sandy Claus."

"Aw," sneered the Kid, "you stink on ice!"

"Have it your own way," Mr. Sears said testily, hurt by his failure. "Move on now. The lights are going out in about five minutes. You wouldn't want to get locked up in here."

"I ain't afraid," the Kid stated. "I ain't afraid of you either."

"You got no call to be afraid of Sandy Claus," Mr. Sears said.

The Kid remained quiet and looked at him carefully. He looked him over from head to foot. When he had finished this close scrutiny his face had changed a little. "All right," he said at last. "Prove it!"

"Prove what?" Mr. Sears inquired. His feet hurt, and any minute he expected Miss Webster to come after him.

"Prove you're Santy Claus."

Mr. Sears was beginning to wish he never had got into this conversation. He would almost have been glad for the sight of Miss Webster's ample and determined figure coming to take him to the shelter. How can you prove something that isn't true? Still, there was a glimmer in the Kid's eyes that kept him from terminating the interview. Whatever it was in the Kid's eyes, he wanted to encourage it.

"All right," he said wearily. "What would it take to prove it?"

"Well," the Kid said cagily, "Santy Claus is supposed to give you something, ain't he? I mean, that's what he's for, ain't it?"

"Yes," Mr. Sears said, almost in a whisper. "That's the story. Now, what is it you want for Christmas?"

Suddenly, the Kid's eyes blazed. His hatchet face lighted up. He smiled. He looked up reverently at the airplane model. He put his hand to his mouth before he spoke, and all the bravado was gone out of him. His small being all but trembled as he said, "I want that."

Mr. Sears' heart sank. He saw himself standing in front of the hardware-store window, so many aeons and aeons ago, looking at the roller skates. They had been only $3.95.

"Oh, you like airplanes," he said.

"Yeah," the Kid breathed. "I like 'em better than anything. I'm gonna fly one—someday. When I get big!"

Mr. Sears had an unannounced onset of his dyspepsia. That is, he got a knot in his throat. Once he had been going to make automobiles when *he* got grown.

"If you're Santy Claus," the Kid said, "I guess you could give it to me, couldn't you?"

Mr. Sears' head began to swim. Now what was he going to do? The thing to do was to come clean. This Kid was no dummy. He would understand the facts of life. You could tell him, right off, that he had been right at the start. That there isn't any Santa Claus. But it was the look in the Kid's eye that stopped him—that tentative, beginning look of something—what was it?—confidence, faith?

"Well," Mr. Sears said, "I couldn't just hand it to you, you know. It ain't Christmas—not till tomorrow night."

"Oh!" The Kid's face hardened.

"You see the way this works," Mr. Sears hastened on, "is like this. I get out my reindeer and stuff, and I could leave it where you live."

"A-hhh," the Kid spat out, "that old baloney."

"You got to give me a chance to prove it," Mr. Sears said. "You got to give me a chance."

Maybe it was the earnestness of his tired old voice. Who knows what it was? The Kid sidled over to him. He looked quizzically into Mr. Sears' eyes. "On the level?" he said.

"Yeah," Mr. Sears said, his mind already made up. "Where do you live?" He dragged toward him the pad and pencil that had been used for the manifold desires of youth.

"It's 1065 Tenth Avenue," the Kid said,

breathing hard. "Fourth floor."

"Tomorrow night," Mr. Sears said.

The store lights winked three times and half of them dimmed. The Kid, now almost beside himself, turned to go.

"Hey," Mr. Sears remembered. "Wait a minute. First you got to be a good boy."

"I been good," he said, slewing his eyes away from Santa Claus.

Mr. Sears held out his hand. "Give it here," he said sternly.

"Huh?"

"Empty 'em out."

The Kid blanched and reached into his lumpy pockets. He removed a baseball, a small and wadded-up pitcher's mitt, and a red muslin sack of marbles, and laid them in Santa Claus' hand.

"Don't ever do that again," Mr. Sears adjured him sternly. "Don't get you no place. No place at all. You hear me?"

The Kid ducked his head. "Okay," he said. "Will—will it make any difference this time?"

"Nope," Mr. Sears said. "Not this time. But don't you forget what I said."

"No, sir," he said, and scurried toward the stairs.

Mr. Sears reflectively examined the small pile of pilfered loot. "You got a hell of a nerve," he said to himself.

The lights dimmed again, and he wearily made

his way to the employees' elevator and divested himself of his Santa Claus regalia. When he got to the exit Miss Webster was pacing the sidewalk.

"What happened to you?" she asked petulantly. "I was beginning to worry."

"Important customer," Mr. Sears said. "Very important."

Christmas Eve was like all Christmas Eves. Harried, last-minute shoppers, tired children, whining and crying, being dragged hastily through the Santa Claus rite. Mr. Sears went through the day in a sort of rosy haze, repeating his part and writing on the slips. All the time his mind was revolving around a desperate plan. He had to get to 1065 Tenth Avenue with a $59.50 plane, the floor sample, and it would take some doing.

But he knew what he was going to do.

When dusk fell on Christmas Eve and the last customer had been propelled out of the building, the Sampson & Cole employees' party was to be held. Mr. Sears was due to make his last appearance as Santa Claus on this occasion. It fitted right into his plans. He was excited as he had not been in years—excited the way he always was before a job. His hands were damp with perspiration, and his mind buzzed.

The day was endless, but eventually it came to a close. The doors were closed, the customers had gone home, and through the store's loud-speaker system the carols began to play. The employees trickled toward the fourth floor, where the cafeteria was. Mr. Sears stayed behind, moving stealthily around his office, smiling to himself. He peered over the hump of papier-mâché, to see that they had all gone. Then, moving very softly, he went to the airplane, snapped the wire that held it, and stuck the plane in his sack, which had been part of his equipment.

"Joy to the world!" pealed the loud-speaker.

The store was empty, except for the crowded fourth floor. Mr. Sears smiled, sidled along the wall in the semi-darkness to the freight elevator. He got in and stopped it at the second floor (piece goods) and got off in the dark. He moved slowly—his eye circling the dimness all the time—to a window, opened it expertly, and climbed out on the fire escape over the alley. He was still wearing his red velvet suit and the whiskers. It tickled him to think of it. It tickled him to think of Miss Webster, who wouldn't be after him until eight o'clock, when the employees' party broke up. Well, he was giving the old girl the slip, all right. He was through with Miss Webster and her watchdogging!

Mr. Sears worked his way down the fire escape with the delicate precision of a practiced hand. His foot touched bottom in the dark alley, and he stopped and looked into the bag to see that the plane was intact. He walked through a maze of alleys and courtyards and back streets, keeping carefully in the shadows. A few people saw him, and their jaws dropped. When this happened he had to lie low.

"Joy to the world!" Mr. Sears murmured in a cracked voice.

It took him almost three hours to work himself to the right block on Tenth Avenue. The slum odors came to him, thick with remembrance. He felt almost like a boy again. He waited a while before he started to climb to the fourth floor. He certainly didn't want to see the Kid. He didn't want to see anybody. He waited until the lights were out in the two-room flat on the fourth floor of the narrow, squalid house. Then he began to climb. At the top landing he stood still a minute, to catch his panting breath, and then tried the door. It was locked, but he had no trouble getting it open. Gently he withdrew the shining bauble from the bag and set it there, inside the room that smelled of stale cabbage and sour beer.

"You old fool," he said to himself.

Mr. Sears' plans had not extended past 1065 Tenth Avenue. He did not know where he was going, especially in this rig. He had to get out of it—get some clothes. It was as bad as convict stripes. Then he thought actively of a saloon— any saloon. But first clothes.

He needn't have worried. He walked hardly

two blocks when a patrol car rolled up to the curb and an officer got out; and Mr. Sears, in a very familiar way, was taken into custody. Miss Webster had been right on the job. When he hadn't put in an appearance after the employees' party, she had gone to the personnel head, and it seemed that Mr. Sears had decamped with the store's property—a red velvet suit, shiny black boots, and an expensive wig. So Miss Webster had given the alarm for a vagrant Santa Claus.

Mr. Sears didn't feel so bad as might have been expected. He was tired, and it might be kind of restful in jail. Besides, it was as much home to him as any place, maybe more so. They usually gave the prisoners turkey on Christmas. In fact, he took it all in his stride, though he knew what it meant. He had broken his parole.

Only he did a strange thing when he was arraigned. He took out sixty dollars, which represented three weeks' salary at Sampson & Cole's, and laid it on the sergeant's blotter. He didn't especially want to—it wasn't his way at all—but he thought about the Tenth Avenue Kid, and he didn't want anything or anyone to take that plane away from him.

"Hrrumph," he said, clearing his throat. "This money belongs to Sampson & Cole. I just bought an airplane over there—one of those toy gimcracks."

He was then led away, still wearing his red

Santa Claus suit.

The desk sergeant stared after him in stupefaction. "That old devil," he said. "Darned if he doesn't look like Santa Claus—to the letter."

And the sergeant was right. For to his other manifest qualifications, Mr. Sears had added something. There was at last a twinkle in his eye.

A Baby Sitter
for Christmas

Mrs. Asa P. Wadlington, relict of Asa P. Wadlington, Sr., a successful insurance broker who had prudently invested in his own commodities, had managed in the half dozen years since the death of her husband to build up a satisfactory life for herself. She had thought, at first, that this would not be possible. She and Asa had been happy together for thirty-odd years and she became aware that his going represented not only the loss of a dearly beloved husband and companion but also the end of that sweet and leisurely cycle of family interdependence and mutual need, of long happy days and peaceful nights in the comfortable, well-worn house of the Wadlingtons. The wheel, of which she was the hub, inexorably began to disintegrate. Her children came of age, and she could tell from the looks on their faces that they were wondering what to do about Mama. This hurt her deeply.

Being a woman of pride and spirit, she set them free. After Asa, Jr., signed on with an oil company and came home, timorous and sweating, to announce that he was shipping out for South America, she did not cry, and when her daughter Elizabeth fell in love with an aircraft executive who lived in Seattle, Washington—about as far away from home as one could get and remain in the United States—Mrs. Wadlington gave her a wedding in the old Wadlington residence, set back from Wilmarth Avenue in its grove of sheltering oaks, and kissed her goodby.

It was the last function ever to be held there. Without bothering to sweep up the rice Mrs. Wadlington sold the house to a construction firm, which immediately razed it and began to rear a skyscraper. Asa and Elizabeth, from Rio and Seattle, wrote anguished letters, not convinced that Mama had done the right thing, fearful that she would never be happy anywhere else, but Mrs. Wadlington, who told herself that it was no longer possible for her to deal in the true nature of happiness, continued to burn her bridges.

She moved into a small flat in an apartment hotel, where the mahogany bedroom furniture of her connubial life looked overpowering, and the Chippendale dining room suite, which had borne so many succulent dinners and supported Wadlingtons since they had sat at the table on the dictionary, had to be abandoned, and the ancient shaggy sofa, on which her family had grown up, could not be got through the door. These things tore at Mrs. Wadlington's heart but she permitted no one to know, for she could not bear sympathy. She, who had always suffered the necessity of choosing serviceable colors, sturdy fabrics and furnishings guaranteed to withstand men, children, and puppies, sublimated her misery by indulging in pale-colored satin damask, perishable carpets, fragile Empire chairs and china. Her little sitting room was as pretty and as smart as a photograph in a magazine. Her friends admired it inordinately.

"Agnes Wadlington is really remarkable," they said all over town.

Mrs. Wadlington was not especially remarkable, if you discount her self-control and the manner in which she grasped independence by the forelock and set it up as a fetish. She was so determined not to be a burden that it became practically necessary to knock her over the head to do her a favor. From the blood and sand and hot sunshine of the arena she moved to a cool, remote, shadowed seat high in the stands, where she reposed in dowager dignity, immune from hurt.

She did not withdraw from the world—far from it! It would have been impossible for this perfect soldier of a woman to fall into idleness.

Her days were full of the made work highly recommended by sociologists and old-age planners, and her interests were diverse and manifold. But she did change. Mrs. Wadlington decided that she was old and that what remained for her was to be as little trouble as possible. To a degree this was forced on her by a civilization which worships youth more than wisdom, but it must be admitted that Mrs. Wadlington fell into this line of reasoning without much of a battle. It was a corollary of the bewilderment of widowhood, the death of love, and the loss of a demanding job. Thrown all at once on her own resources, Mrs. Wadlington chose dignity and loneliness in preference to whining and compromise which she deplored in contemporaries of like estate. She said, over and over, that young people must be left to their own devices and that she had had her share of child-rearing.

Superficially it might have seemed that Mrs. Wadlington's children neglected her, but the truth was that both Elizabeth and Asa adored their mother and missed her much more than she admitted missing them. Life had flung them far from home, but the warmth and solidarity of their old family circle went with them wherever they traveled. They were nonplused that she was so able to endure without them.

On the infrequent occasions when Mrs. Wadlington could be persuaded to travel to Seattle, she was a credit as a house-guest. Her clothes were smart, her conversation informed, and their friends thought her charming. She never criticized nor offered her daughter suggestions about anything. But there was something new and unsatisfactory about the relationship. Elizabeth used to cry bitterly after her mother had taken her well-timed departure, for she had the feeling that she had been entertaining an elegant stranger. Mrs. Wadlington was so sensible about everything that Elizabeth, remembering the cracking good quarrels, crises, and emotions of the past, was at a loss to understand what had happened to her.

Mrs. Wadlington found these visits a great strain. Naturally after a few days in her daughter's ménage, she would be bursting with advice, counsel, condemnation, and helpless love, touched by Elizabeth's inept struggles with housekeeping and motherhood, chagrined with how little she had managed to teach her, and otherwise full of the voice of experience, which she felt called upon to quell. She was drawn to Joe, her son-in-law, a large, awkward man who reminded her of Asa, but she was so incapable of encroaching upon the lives of this new circle that she never said anything. She knew that if she opened her mouth she would not be able to climb back upon the pedestal where she would be a burden to no one, with the possible exception of herself.

Time passed slowly for Mrs. Wadlington, where once it had run away, in spite of the busy round of clubs and church and the reasonable social life of a woman her age. She spent some of it on herself. Her hands recovered from years of housework and gardening and looked rather pretty and useless. Her coiffure bore signs of a modest blue rinse, and no hair of it was ever out of place. Her clothes were distinguished, and she was given to little flowery toques and dove gray, and when she drove out in her elderly Buick people said, "There goes Mrs. Wadlington of the Haverford Arms. Isn't she lovely?"

Mrs. Wadlington naturally derived some satisfaction from this masquerade she had been at considerable pains to create, and was bucked up when it was reported that a young physician she had met on one of her charitable rounds reported that she was the most perfectly adjusted woman of her age he had ever met. She did not admit that she would have traded all her carefully acquired loveliness and adjustment for one good domestic crisis in the old house on Wilmarth Street. But need it be said, those days were gone forever.

It was only around Christmas that she actually ceased to be Mrs. Wadlington of the Haverford Arms and became Aggie, human being, at least in her heart. Mrs. Wadlington scored herself for this weakness, but no matter how her mind insisted that Christmas was simply another day, preceded by hysteria, tinsel, and twaddle and succeeded by indigestion and fatigue, she was aware that

Christmas was also the flushed faces and trusting eyes of children, the smell of profligate spice, drying spruce, and roasting turkey, the present too expensive for the budget, the tangle of tissue paper and extravagant ribbons going up in smoke on the Yule log, the wild confusion of chilly dawn, the busy doorbell, the indescribable weariness which is the price of love.

About the first of December she always began to feel moody, and in the course of some routine pursuit she would remember how Asa had fallen off the stepladder, through the Christmas tree, and smashed the bottle of perfume he had saved lunch money for weeks to buy her, and how she had sat down on the floor, too tired to weep, and got the hysterical giggles; how she had cradled Asa's head in her lap and kissed away his rotund curses. Or how Elizabeth, having proudly forsworn Santa Claus, had bellowed and yelped when she did not find a lumpy stocking hanging on her bed post on Christmas morning, or how Asa, Jr., swollen with his first pocket money, had bought her an egg-beater as a present.

"Nonsense," Mrs. Wadlington would scold herself stoutly, when she found she was about to give in to sentiment and have a good cry. But she did feel it was unfair of memory to go on scribbling these hieroglyphs on a slate she had managed to wipe so clean.

She made various plans to outwit the fissure in her iron personality. She even tried visiting the children, but it was all so strange and different from the past, and she missed Asa so abominably that she gave that up. Every year Elizabeth inaugurated a campaign to get Mama to come, but Mrs. Wadlington, ever resourceful, had planned a cruise or was going to Miami with a friend or had something else in mind. Mrs. Wadlington, reviewing the dreary hotel rooms she had passed Christmas in, told herself that she was just a fool and this year she would stay at home, where she was comfortable, at least.

She then began to impose upon the unconquerable season of Christmas the petty outlines of her new life. She bought at the florist's a little crystalline tree and trimmed it with new and modern baubles, which had no concern with the lopsided cedars, with the old, moth-eaten angel, and the toy soldier, from which the paint had disappeared, that had been the standard equipment of Christmas trees on Wilmarth Avenue. Though her Christmas tree was exquisite she could not bear to look at it, and she eventually gave up the thought of having dinner in the flat (where the oven was too small for anything anyway) and made a reservation in the hotel dining room for Estelle Winters, another widow, and herself. She wrapped her gifts in the new turquoise and fuchsia trappings, which seemed so far away from the red and white of old, and contributed a sum of money to the Salvation Army. All these things efficiently dispatched, she sat down to wait for the bitter day, feeling very cold and modern.

As the time drew near, she became more and more moody and even went so far as to drive down Wilmarth Avenue and stare at the old address, which held the skyscraper as remote from the past as she was herself. She took to lying awake nights and found that she was talking to herself.

"Now see here," Mrs. Wadlington admonished herself one morning, "this has got to stop, or you'll be sick, and then you will be a burden."

"But I'm so lonely," Aggie said tearfully to Mrs. Wadlington. "I don't care."

"Don't act like a child!" Mrs. Wadlington muttered to her alter ego.

"Child!" whined Aggie. "But Christmas . . ."

Mrs. Wadlington pulled herself together with one final remark. "It's all right to talk to yourself," she opined to the empty room, "but when you start answering yourself back something must be done."

That evening her eye fell on the desperate want ad.

Wanted. Baby sitter for two children. For Christmas Eve. Price no object. Stanton 4906.

Mrs. Wadlington told herself that such a notion was madness, folded the newspaper, and went out to the movies. Having reconnoitered the situation throughout a double feature, advising herself that it was ridiculous, that she did not need the money, that she couldn't bear strange houses, that she hadn't been around children in years and wouldn't know what to do with them, and what people would think, she went home and telephoned Stanton 4906.

"Oh, what a relief!" cried young Mrs. Vernon Fielding on the other end of the wire. "We've got this party, and the nurse has left. And of course every baby sitter I know has been engaged for Christmas Eve since August! Isn't it marvelous you're free."

Mrs. Wadlington, struck with the thought of how free she really was and how far short of marvelous freedom could fall, said diffidently, "I'm afraid I haven't had much experience."

"Oh, anybody can sit," Mrs. Fielding said. "You don't drink, do you?"

"Certainly not," Mrs. Wadlington said, horrified.

"Can happen," Mrs. Fielding returned, unabashed, from the wealth of her experience with sitters. "If you could come around six—I'll have to dress. Shall I send for you?"

"Heavens, no," Mrs. Wadlington said with more heat than she had mustered in years. "I'm not decrepit."

"You never know," said Mrs. Fielding airily, and gave her the address.

Mrs. Wadlington hung up and sat down. Her knees were nervous. She felt old and inadequate, and she could not imagine why she had sold herself for five dollars. Indeed, she could not imagine why she had mixed herself up in such a situation at all. To have admitted the desperation of her desire to fondle a child was more than she could face. In spite of the dubious beginning of this adventure, she entertained a vision of herself telling a beautiful story to two blond tots in immaculate sleepers. She went out and bought a copy of Clement Moore's poem and refreshed her memory. All week she reveled in ridiculous dreams and plans.

The Fieldings lived in one of those suburbs which bristle with new brick houses and the way-ward beginnings of elaborate gardens which in-dicate that the man of the house is moving upward in his business and living beyond his means. When Mrs. Wadlington bore up the walk in the dusk of Christmas Eve, Mr. Vernon Fielding, trying to fasten his collar button, was looking out the window.

"Who's that?" he said.

"It's probably the baby sitter," Martha Fielding shouted from the shower. "Will you go down, Vern?"

"Looks more like a duchess," said Vernon. "Where'd you find her?"

"Newspaper ad," said Martha. "I hope she's clean and kind."

"Foxy grandma," said Vernon, and clattered down the stairs. "How do you do," he said.

"Please come in."

Mrs. Wadlington stepped over a tricycle, a welter of building blocks, a nauseous looking paintbox, and a legless doll.

"Please excuse this mess. They won't put anything away."

She would have liked to ask why, but forbore, since she hesitated to get off on the wrong foot professionally. "Well, it is Christmas," said Mrs. Wadlington.

"My mother would have beat my ears down," Vernon confided. "But they have theories about such things now. Wounds their psyches or something."

"Really," said Mrs. Wadlington.

"Yep, you have to keep them adjusted. I'm not sure to what."

Mrs. Wadlington recollected that she too was adjusted and began to fear the worst.

Martha Fielding came running down the stairs. She was a pretty, dark girl in a red taffeta dress. "Oh, here you are," she said without looking at Mrs. Wadlington. "The children are just having their supper. They have to be washed before they go to bed. They ought to go to sleep straight off."

They went into a small morning room, where two owlish young were dawdling over their food. "Robin, Pammie, this is the nice lady who's— going to put you to bed."

"I'm not going to bed," announced Robin. He looked, to the best of Mrs. Wadlington's judgment, about six or seven. He was a small, wiry, darkling creature, entirely unlike the blond curlyhead Mrs. Wadlington had envisioned.

"Waaaaah!" mourned Pamela, and climbed down from her chair to traipse after her mother.

"Now, Pammie, don't get applesauce on my dress," said Mrs. Fielding. "Finish your supper."

"I'm going with you," stated Pamela.

"Now, dear, I've explained it all to you," said Mrs. Fielding, and sat down to reason with the four-year-old mentality.

"Come on, Marty," shouted Mr. Fielding from the hallway. "We're late."

"I don't like her," said Robin, pointing to Mrs. Wadlington who was cowering on the outskirts of this scene. "Where's Mrs. Fox?"

"You know how children are," said Martha, smiling at Mrs. Wadlington. "So frank. He'll come around in a few minutes."

Mrs. Wadlington did not feel so sure, but she gathered herself together.

"Marty!" bellowed Mr. Fielding.

Mrs. Fielding picked her way through the assorted debris in the foyer and thrust her arms into her coat. Robin danced around the couple shooting an imaginary gun and shouting, "You're dead!" Pamela resolved on simple screaming. Mrs. Wadlington felt herself getting a headache.

So began the reign of terror.

When she was able to corral the wailing Pamela and return to the supper table she began a desperate effort to woo the boy who was kicking the paintbox around the living room.

"Come finish your supper, dear," Mrs. Wadlington invited.

"You can't make me," Robin paused to intone.

"They don't eat enough to keep a bird alive," said the maid, who was moving around the table. "Have to beg 'em. I call it a shame. Children hungry all over the place."

"Keep an eye on her," said Mrs. Wadlington and retreated to the living room. A Christmas tree, rather sketchily trimmed, was standing in one corner. "What a beautiful tree," said Mrs. Wadlington without conviction.

"It's mine," said Robin. "It's not Pammie's."

"I don't think Santa Claus would like to hear you say that," Mrs. Wadlington reproved.

"Aaaah, there's no such thing as Santa Claus," Robin Fielding said.

Mrs. Wadlington was stunned. In some ridiculous way she had been trying to find Santa Claus herself, and this wistfulness had inspired the miserable circumstance she now found herself in. "Well," she said stiffly, "if you don't believe in him he probably doesn't believe in you." With this she retired to find that Pamela had put her hand in the mashed potatoes and was now using them for finger-painting.

"Pamela!" rebuked Mrs. Wadlington, her voice rising.

"You're supposed to reason with them,"

reminded the maid.

Mrs. Wadlington summoned what was left of her reason.

Robin, deserted, inched into the room. "What makes your hair blue?" he asked.

Mrs. Wadlington winced. The rinse had always made her nervous. She would have liked to retort, "Because that's the color of it," but she felt it was beneath her dignity and not strictly the truth. "I wash it in blue water," she stated.

"Now we're all going to have a bath," she said. "And then I'll tell you a lovely story."

"Not me," Robin said. "I don't like stories."

"Then you don't have to listen," said Mrs. Wadlington. "I'll tell it to Pammie."

"I don't like stories either," said Pam.

"Copycat!" shouted Robin. They launched into a free-for-all.

For the first time in years, Mrs. Wadlington felt hurt seeping into her. She was being rejected by two infants. That's what came of permitting yourself to be rejected. Nobody wanted to hear her story. "I'm really childish," she thought. "An old woman!"

The two of them were rolling on the floor, breathing hard. "Ouch, that hurts. Pam, stop! She's biting me," howled Robin.

"Get up!" she ordered, and stopped to separate them. Robin landed a kick on her shins. Mrs. Wadlington felt as if she would like to return it, but instead she ignored him and picked up

Pamela. "Let me down!" bleated Pamela. "I don't *know* you."

"My name is Mrs. Wadlington," said Mrs. Wadlington progressively, "and I am going to give you a bath."

"No!"

Robin trailed her up the stairs. "We didn't hang up our stockings yet," he ventured.

Mrs. Wadlington seized on this. "Not until after you've both had a bath," she said.

Robin broke for the other bathroom but Pamela was not so easily quelled. During a tussle in which her back ached, her hair began to string down, and she got a handful of soap bubbles in the mouth, Mrs. Wadlington began to worry about the peace and quiet at the other end of the hall. The moment she was able to dry off the squirming seal of a child and get her into a towel she hastened to the scene of Robin's operations.

In the midst of a shambles of steam, bubble-bath water, and damp linen stood the naked imp. He was pouring ink into the tub.

"Robin!" squeaked Mrs. Wadlington. "What are you doing?"

He grinned like a satyr. "I'm going to have blue hair," he said.

Mrs. Wadlington longed to attack him in the proper spot, rendered especially vulnerable by his nudity, but there was something about this skinny child's body, about the hyena grin, that made her want to snicker. She fled to the hall and laughed as she had not laughed since before Asa died.

"Let that water out and start over," she commanded, when she had got her face straight. "Reason!" she snorted to herself. Her dove-gray dress was covered with water, soap, and ink. Her shin smarted. But it took her back.

She never knew quite how she got them clothed and remained in her right mind. Robin, with expected cupidity, was intent on hanging up his father's golf sock and considerable dissuasion was required. They seemed sobered by the ritual of the stockings, and Pammie leaned against her when the two small stockings were affixed to the mantel. Robin stood at her knee. Mrs. Wadlington softened. There was something forlorn about the three of them, she thought—somebody else's children, somebody else's grandmother.

"What am I doing here?" she asked herself. "And why aren't *they* here?" Why was the world so bent on independence—so afraid of ties and being bound together. People were bound together by the very fact of being on the strange earth. Wasn't it lonely enough to be a human being, without constantly insisting on gratifying the selfish will? Wasn't it less independence and more interdependence that was needed, from birth to death, from sea to sea? What was everybody afraid of? What was she afraid of? The heart?

"You could tell us the story now?" Robin gave in.

She got them in their beds and settled down.

She had never been so eloquent. Mrs. Wadlington's rendition of *The Night Before Christmas* deserved to go down in history and indeed, it did. When she had finished and the last imaginary reindeer had taken off through the sky, Pamela was asleep, her long lashes lying on her appleblossom cheeks. The boy lay quiescent, his dark eyes shining in the night light.

She tiptoed out to look over the chaos of the bathrooms. They were an affront to her tidy nature and a challenge to Aggie Wadlington. As little as that young woman deserved it, she pinned up her dress and went in search of scrubbing materials. In her rummaging in closets she came upon the trove of expensive presents. Everything dear to the childish heart seemed to be collected there, but Mrs. Wadlington shook her head. She was beginning to believe that you couldn't buy anything you really wanted. She had been trying for years.

She attacked the bathrooms with unnecessary vigor, and it was almost midnight when she shook out the last towel. "Sitter!" said Mrs. Wadlington. "A fine misnomer." She sank down on the sofa in the disordered living room to regard the stockings and the dismal little tree, but before she had drawn an easy breath, she was startled by the loud peal of the doorbell.

A policeman was standing there.

"Good evening, lady," he said. "My name's Mitchell. I don't want to scare you, but there seems to be a kid out on your roof."

"What!" shrieked Mrs. Wadlington.

"Now take it easy. My partner and I—we're the Safety Squad—we're covering our beat, flashing the light around, and it picks up what looks like a little boy crawling around up there. Reckon he's looking for Santy Claus. Now . . ."

"Robin!" moaned Mrs. Wadlington, and bolted up the stairs. His bed was empty and the window stood open. "What shall we do?" Mrs. Wadlington wrung her pretty, useless hands together.

"Now you just keep calm," Mr. Mitchell begged. "You go downstairs and watch him. I'll shinny up there and keep him company. My partner has gone for a hook and ladder. As long as he's not scared, everything will be all right!"

"Merciful heavens, I know I'm going to faint!"

"Now none of that. He's all right as long as he don't get afraid. You go down and encourage him if he acts skittish."

Dying a hundred small, unimportant deaths, Mrs. Wadlington hurtled down the stairs and out on the lawn. The child was edging unconcernedly along the ridgepole toward the chimney, his slender frame silhouetted against the starry sky.

"I cannot look," Mrs. Wadlington decided but found that she could not stop. Robin moved with the nimble grace of a small animal, while the shadow of Patrolman Mitchell swung itself over the gable and began to progress with clumsy, adult caution over the steep incline of the roof toward his quarry.

"Dear God," prayed Mrs. Wadlington incoherently, "do not let anything happen to this incredible boy and I will teach him a good lesson!"

The street was fortunately quiet, but as the child reached the chimney, a window was flung up next door and a man said, "What's going on?" The fire wagon swooped up noiselessly, and a squad of men brought the long ladder and set it against the roof's edge. A little knot of people collected and watched the drama in stricken silence.

Robin reconnoitered the chimney with thoroughness and was just turning to go back down the ridgepole toward the roof slope, when Mitchell swung his leg over and sat astride the pole to block his passage.

"See anything of him?" he inquired in a normal voice.

"Nope," said Robin. "I think it's too little."

Mrs. Wadlington gasped, and there was a sibilant sigh from the stunned watchers.

"I'm getting cold," Robin announced.

"There's a ladder," said Mitchell. "I reckon it would be faster." He seized his prey around the waist like a sack of meal and swung over to the gable where the fire ladder rested.

"Put me down," Robin commanded distinctly. "You leave me alone."

"You're in the hands of the police. Pipe down."

"You got a badge?" asked Robin.

"Here you are," Mitchell said, and handed Mrs. Wadlington her shivering charge. Mrs. Wadlington, still amazed that she hadn't fainted dead away, rolled him in a blanket and took him to the kitchen where she heated milk. She did not speak.

"What you going to do?" Robin finally asked her, rigid with defiance.

"Drink this," said Mrs. Wadlington, "and then I propose to warm you up in a rather old-fashioned manner."

Robin bore up in good order, seeming to be somewhat relieved by the broad palm of discipline and without need of reasoning. He understood it perfectly. When he had stopped snuffling, he leaned against her.

"You could tell me another story," he offered.

"Not tonight," said Mrs. Wadlington. "Some other time."

"You could hold me, then," he searched for the proper olive branch. "If you want to."

She gathered him up, the skinny little realist, and her arms tightened around him. He nestled against her. His dark, bristly head burrowed the arc of her shoulder. She wished, idiotically, that the chimney had been bigger, that just for a few hours he could have believed in something beyond his own puny power. Poor little man, perhaps he too had wished it in that inquiring mind, born of an unsentimental century.

Mrs. Wadlington had just lugged her sleeping

burden back to bed when Mr. and Mrs. Vernon Fielding burst in, white to the eyes. Rumor had apparently reached them in the midst of merriment.

"What happened?" they babbled. "Where is he? Is he safe?"

"No credit to you," declared Mrs. Wadlington, and rolled up her verbal sleeves. Mrs. Wadlington's play-by-play account of the events of the night, liberally editorialized with her views of the present-day world, was a masterpiece of rhetoric.

"How dare you strike my son!" broke in Mrs. Fielding midway in this account.

Mrs. Wadlington was instantly reduced to personalities. She had been looking for an opening.

"See here," said Vernon. "Don't you speak to my wife like that. You've got her crying!"

"Well," said Mrs. Wadlington, her dudgeon mounting, "I'm glad to see there is some kind of mutual feeling, some family solidarity around here. I was beginning to think it was every man for himself."

"We won't need you any further," Vernon said loftily. "You may go. There, there, Marty. Everything's all right."

"Everything's all wrong!" Mrs. Wadlington contradicted. "With everybody!" With this acid sally she jammed her toque on her head crookedly, rubbed her shin, and went out the door, a tattered frigate but ready to sail on.

"Good grief," said Martha five minutes later. "I forgot to pay her!"

Mrs. Wadlington dragged herself into the Haverford Arms, slunk through the lobby, for she was no fit sight for that conservative hostelry, and gained her ivory tower. For a moment it looked peaceful and inviting but when she caught sight of herself in the great gilt mirror over the fireplace, she could not believe it belonged to her. She sank into one of the satin chairs to gain strength to go on. She was so tired. While she stared into space, her eye fell on the yellow telegram envelope propped against the Meissen figurine where the maid had left it.

Mrs. Wadlington got up, put out a limp and grimy hand, and eventually managed the impetus to open it. It was from Seattle.

Dear Mama we cannot bear for you to be alone Christmas. Flying down with the children. Love, Elizabeth and Joe.

Mrs. Wadlington, in whom the Christmas spirit had simmered down considerably, reeled at the implications of these words. Christmas was tomorrow—today! They were probably on the way, maybe almost here. In this four-room flat! And then the memory of Robin Fielding in her arms recurred to her.

"Why, that's wonderful," Mrs. Wadlington

thought. And she reflected with shame that her grandchildren had never spent a Christmas in the town of their forefathers, that she had never asked them. It might have occurred to her that Elizabeth had lived most of her life in this city and that perhaps she wanted to come home for the holidays.

"I'll get a larger tree," Mrs. Wadlington planned. "I'll cook a turkey somehow. I'll have a party!"

Happiness ran through her veins, warm, golden, like wine. She moved around the room making plans, and at length reflectively began to set her china treasures off the tables up onto high shelves. "Perhaps a small switch," she murmured. "Just a tiny little one."

This remark could only be construed to mean that Aggie was back in business.

Uncle Edgar
And the
Reluctant Saint

Almost every grown person remembers with tender sadness the year he found out who Santa Claus was. Because after that Christmas, no Christmas was ever the same again, nor was anything else. The world, held at bay by the gentle legend and unshaken trust of childhood, thereafter encroached upon the virgin country and all the things which had been taken on faith became suspect. Something went out of the heart and, for the time being, there was nothing to put in its place.

I was luckier than most. When Santa Claus departed my life, Uncle Edgar came into it in a new and significant way.

When I was a little girl, I had a whole passel of

uncles, some satisfactory and some only fair, but Uncle Edgar was the one we never mentioned outside the home. Uncle Edgar did not turn up at family gatherings, except in conversation where aunts, knitting fast and speaking through compressed lips, referred to him as a scapegrace and a black sheep; uncles, tamping down their pipe tobacco and scratching matches on the seats of their pants, opined that it did look as if Ed had played the fool long enough, and even my grandmother, with a hint of tears behind her mild blue eyes, admitted wistfully that she wished Eddie would marry some good girl and settle down.

Uncle Edgar was, naturally, the uncle who interested me most. I tried to fit him to the various descriptions I heard around family conclaves but he did not seem to be much like anything they said. I knew Uncle Edgar, for he occasionally turned up at our house, unannounced, in the middle of the night, wanting lodging. My mother would have to get up and fly around, putting fresh linen on the spare-room bed and dragging out my father's best pajamas, while my father lay there muttering condemnation. These occasions filled me with such excitement I could scarcely sleep. I knew that in the morning there would be hot popovers and Uncle Edgar would be sitting across the table with the sun flaming in his shock of red curly hair and burnishing the sunburned pillar of his throat, while my mother plied him with her most ambitious cooking.

He was a lean man—lean and hungry. His hips were narrow and his legs, slightly bowed, were thin and muscled; his shoulders were wide but without surplus flesh, as if they were the base of an inverted triangle of bone. There was nothing soft about him, except his face, which had a way of looking startled like a small boy's. His eyes were very blue and a little bewildered. His red hair fell down on his freckled forehead and his nose quivered when he got mad, which was often. His mouth might have been gentle but he seemed determined to make it surly and he kept his jaw jutting forward by some conscious effort. My mother said the root of her brother's trouble was stubbornness, but my father said he was just plain wild.

I felt a kindred feeling for Uncle Edgar, for I too was said to have a trouble rooted in stubbornness, and I used to stare at him while he ate breakfast, trying to ferret out the nature of his wildness. He was interesting to look at anyway, for he did not wear a stiff collar or a fawn-colored coat or a derby hat like my father. He wore an old flannel shirt, open at the neck, a tooled, russet leather belt, mounted with Mexican dollars, faded blue breeches, and a pair of high-heeled black boots with a small, neat pair of roweled spurs. Uncle Edgar was a cowboy.

Nobody in the family wanted Uncle Edgar to be a cowboy, for this was the time when the ploughshares were beginning to turn over the great ranches and make cotton fields out of them and all the cowboys who had a wink of sense were climbing off their horses and going into professions and businesses that had a future. Uncle Edgar, however, had never been one to listen to counsel or take orders, and no sooner did the family decide to make him a lawyer than he peremptorily left home and got a job punching cattle for thirty dollars a month. My mother was the only member of the family who stood by him. He was her youngest brother, and, as she said, you can drive a horse to water but you can't make him drink. That was Uncle Edgar all over. Whatever he did, he had to do it himself.

I do not know what species of trouble Uncle Edgar had got into but cowboys were wild roisterers in those days, when the stabler members of their ilk had begun to desert the trade for the ways of town-life and church-going. Uncle Edgar had a big bay horse and a pistol in a leather holster and I suppose he must have shot up something one Saturday night in an excess of youthful spirits. He never talked about himself or his exploits, even to my mother, for he was a silent man, absurdly bashful to be grown, sometimes stumbling over his own feet or the furniture when he got caught in a house. I used to hear my mother begging him to control his temper and not get in any more fights, because the sheriff was already down on him.

Such was Uncle Edgar. He was especially shy

in my presence. He always called me Sis and just before he would disappear for another long period of time, he would press a silver dollar into my grimy palm, adjuring me to buy candy with it, and then back off, usually falling over a chair in the process.

I loved him.

I did not know what Uncle Edgar really thought of me until the Christmas I was six years old. I had been sent on a visit to my grandmother just before the holidays while my father and mother made a flying business trip to St. Louis. My grandmother had expected to accompany me home, but the day before Christmas Eve, she had come down with sciatica and could scarcely move. Since it was unthinkable I should spend Christmas away from home (how would Santa Claus know where I was?) there was a great stir and at length it was decided by Grandma and two uncles and three aunts that I would have to make the four-hour day trip on the train alone, entrusted to the tender care of Mr. Smith, the conductor of the Brazos Valley & Central passenger train. If I had started out to cross the Great Plains solo and afoot, there could not have been more confusion, brow-wrinkling, and general concern.

As a matter of fact, the Brazos Valley & Central passenger train (once per day) ran over a spur of some hundred miles so slowly that any horse could outrun it. Mr. Smith, who had been on the train since the spur was built, had lifted me on it and off it since I had been a babe in arms (the whole family lived in various small towns up and down this spur), and his celluloid collar and walrus moustache were as familiar to me as the characteristics of any uncle. I was also personally acquainted with Mr. Bolander, the engineer who sometimes waved his bandanna to me when we drove down to the station on Sunday evenings to watch the train pass through, and Chester, the brakeman, had once let me hold his lantern. It seemed unlikely that I could be safer in my mother's arms than on the Brazos Valley & Central. I personally had no qualms about the matter and indeed, I looked forward to the journey with somewhat ungrateful pleasure. I was almost glad sciatica had come along.

Nobody else shared my aplomb. Aunt Josephine buttoned me into my moleskin coat with the braided frogs and tied my brown velvet bonnet on with lengthy instructions about how to divest myself of these outer garments once I got in that overheated coach. I had been taking off my own coat for years and was very bored. Aunt Eliza handed me a groaning shoebox, filled with enough lunch to feed several men, though I would be home well before supper. Uncle Garland gave me a dollar bill, which Aunt Mae pinned with a safety pin to the lining of my brown silk purse. Grandmother, lying stiffly in bed, begged me to be a good girl and not to speak to strangers. Then

Uncle Whit came, whirled me off to the station in a hired hack, bought my ticket, and held a whispered conference with Mr. Smith as soon as the train, heaving and sighing, paused at the weather-beaten station. Mr. Smith nodded his head over and over and I was handed up into a coach and Uncle Whit followed me with my suitcase. He put the bag in the rack overhead, settled me firmly on a red plush seat and delicately pushed the white granite spittoon out of sight under the opposite seat.

"Now you stay right here," Uncle Whit said, as if I were a baby, "and before you know it, your papa will be taking you off the train. And if you want anything, ask Mr. Smith. Don't move unless you ask Mr. Smith!"

It occurred to me that there were some things I could not possibly ask Mr. Smith, but I didn't want to unnerve Uncle Whit any more than he was, so I said, "All right."

Uncle Whit bade me good-bye and after one more conference with Mr. Smith, he swung himself off the train and came back beside the window where I was sitting and continued his worried gesticulations to the effect that I was to stay in that seat until my journey was over. I kept nodding my head up and down to try to reassure him until, with many a creak and groan which had justly earned the Brazos Valley & Central the title of "Wooden Axle," the train pulled away from the station and picked its lackadaisical way across the prairie between the clumps of prickly pear and mesquite trees.

I originally had had no intention of obeying my elders' orders once I got out of sight of them, but as the train hove away and I looked around the car I began to feel small and serious. Not only were there no other children in the car, there were no ladies. I had had some hazy and high-colored notion that the Brazos Valley & Central would be full of merry progeny about my age and that I could run amok, having no grown-up around with the authority to quell me. But it was Christmas Eve and everybody who was going to spend Christmas with his grandmother had already gone. There was not even a stray mother around in case something terrible happened.

I craned my neck toward the door, for I was glued to my seat by this startling realization, and looked backward toward the other car. It was a smoker and naturally no lady would be caught dead in there. The car ahead was the mail car and I could see the government man in a green eye-shade and a black apron, handling the mailbags. The car ahead of that, I knew, was the baggage car. The Brazos Valley & Central boasted only four cars. I was adrift in a world of men.

At once I began to remember what everybody had told me to do, so I got up and took off my coat, folded it neatly, divested myself of my bonnet, and sat down again, clutching my purse and my lunchbox. Nobody said anything to me, so I was saved the necessity of not speaking to strangers. I gazed around the coach at its occupants, which did not add to my comfort. There was a rough-looking man in the front seat—he had long hair and a beard and an old flat hat on, very greasy and dirty. I took him to be a sheepherder. He had a tremendous sack of wool. Across the aisle and down one seat there was a small swarthy man with heavy eyebrows, piercing black eyes, and a moustache. He had a large pack on the seat beside him and I recognized him as a peddler, one of those itinerant vendors who used to travel the West with a stock of indispensable merchandise and shoddy pretties which brought cheer to many a hard-bitten rancher's wife.

The seat directly in front of me was filled up with the bulk of a fat man in a black alpaca suit, wearing a white shirt, a black string tie, and a large, fawn-colored Stetson hat. On the lapel of his shiny black suit was pinned a glistening silver star. His coat was unbuttoned, and stretched across his pendulous stomach was a heavy gold watch fob with an unusually fierce-looking elk's tooth depending from it. In spite of his heavy jowls and beetling black eyebrows, he was a dapper man, and his black, high-topped boots were fastidiously shined. He was dressed up for Christmas.

As the train ground along with a seasick motion, there was no sound but the creaking of the worn wheels on the track and occasional shouts from the smoker where the other occupants of the train were smoking black cigars and playing faro, and for all I know, nipping Christmas cheer out of a bottle.

I was very lonely and stiff from sitting so still and I began to wonder what had become of Mr. Smith. I felt that soon I must look on a familiar face. Just as I began to get really restless, the fat man in the seat ahead folded his newspaper and stood up, probably bent on going into the smoker. As he came abreast of me he paused and said: "Hello, Kid."

Grandma had told me not to speak to strangers, so I dropped my eyes and toyed with the handle of my purse.

"Aren't you Charlie Grant's kid?" the man asked in his deep, bass voice, and I cut my eyes toward him and nodded, but as I did so, I read the legend on the silver star. "S-h-e-r-i-f-f" it said. Here, here in the flesh, was the arch enemy of Uncle Edgar. A shiver ran over me. Any enemy of Uncle Edgar's was bound to be an enemy of mine.

I looked busily out the window.

"Looky here," the sheriff said. He obviously thought he had a great way with children. "What's the matter? Has the cat got your tongue?"

I was moved to stick it out at him for graphic proof that he was mistaken, but controlled the impulse and simply shook my head and kept looking out the window. He put a heavy hand on my shoulder and turned me around so that the elk's tooth just grazed my nose and I jumped.

"Scaredy cat, ain't you?" he said.

"I am not," I blazed. "I'm not supposed to speak to strangers."

"I'm no stranger," he said. "I've known your Daddy since he was so high—no bigger'n you. You look exactly like him. The spitten image."

"Well, Grandma told me . . ."

"Know her, too," the sheriff remarked. "Fine old lady."

Mr. Smith came by at this point, mumbling unintelligibly the name of the next village where the train stopped. I felt great relief.

"How you doing, Sis?" Mr. Smith asked.

"Just fine," I said in a thin voice.

"Well, well, Charlie Grant's kid," the sheriff said to Mr. Smith. "I remember mighty well the day he was no bigger than this urchin."

I didn't know what "urchin" was but I didn't like the sound of it. I glowered, now that Mr. Smith's kindly presence was there to protect me.

"Yep," Mr. Smith said. "This is little Sissy Grant. She's been down to visit her grandma. Her folks are going to take her off the train in Porterfield."

"Well, I declare," the sheriff said with heavy jocularity. "A Christmas package. Why isn't she riding up in the mail car with the parcel post?"

Mr. Smith smiled benignly, somewhat pleased to be engaged in conversation by the man of the law.

"Tell you what we could do," the sheriff pursued. "Write out a tag and tie it around her neck and let Jack toss her in the mailbag for Porterfield."

I was not unaccustomed to the teasing ways of adults with children, but this was a notion which sounded pretty plausible to me and I began to feel qualms. I had no doubt that this horrible sheriff could arrange it. I inched away from them and pressed my face to the windowpane.

Sheriff Bonner, for that was his name, yawned, stretched, and dropped into the seat that faced mine. Mr. Smith went on into the smoker to announce the name of the town which everybody on the Brazos Valley & Central knew anyway. The train was imperceptibly slowing to a stop at the dull-red station where a little knot of people were waiting to get on.

I gave them my complete attention.

"Never saw such a young'un," the sheriff said, winking at the peddler. "The only lady on the train and I am getting no place fast."

The swarthy man stretched his mouth into a tired smile. The sheriff continued to harass me.

"You know what's liable to happen," he said. "When you get to Porterfield, I bet old Charlie Grant won't be at the station to meet you."

"He will too!" I sputtered.

"Been gone, hasn't he? Been up to St. Louis on a trip Mr. Smith said. How do you know he's home yet."

"He is, he is!" I cried passionately. "My daddy *will* meet me."

"Bet you a jawbreaker he won't," Mr. Bonner said.

"You wait and see!" I threatened.

"Like as not he and your mamma are having such a good time in St. Louis they won't remember anything about you," the sheriff said, noticing that he had discovered a hole in my armor.

My distress suffused me. I had been homesick at Grandma's. That week had seemed like a year. Maybe St. Louis was a wonderful place. Maybe they had forgotten me. But at Christmas—they couldn't. They couldn't! I defended them hotly against my aroused suspicion. I wanted to cry but I felt too old for that. My chest felt tight and funny. Perspiration broke out on my forehead. I did not know which way to turn and then I looked up and there was Uncle Edgar, standing at the door of the coach, his red hair tousled, his face flushed, a crooked smile on his lips. He must have got on at the last station. I don't know where he was going on Christmas Eve. I doubt if he did.

"Uncle Edgar," I cried and left the seat and ran to him.

"Why Sissy," he said. "What are you doing on here? Is Mamma with you?"

"I'm by myself," I said importantly. "Grandma got sciatica."

We got back to my seat and Uncle Edgar

looked down from his six-foot eminence on the sheriff.

"Who's your friend?" Uncle Edgar snarled.

"Hello, Ed," Sheriff Bonner said. "Keeping yourself straight, I hope."

"No credit to you," Uncle Edgar said. "How do you happen to be hanging around Sissy?"

"She's in my custody," Sheriff Bonner said jovially.

"I am not," I put in. "Uncle Whit gave me to Mr. Smith, the conductor."

"You better not let me catch you picking on this kid," Uncle Edgar said thickly. "Keep your teasing to yourself!"

"Are you threatening me?" Sheriff Bonner inquired humorously. "Sounds like liquor talking."

"You can take it anyway you want to," Uncle Edgar said and started for the smoker.

"Keep a civil tongue in your head, my boy. Remember there's a lady present."

"You remember it," Uncle Edgar said and stalked toward the smoker.

"Uncle Edgar!" I cried. "Don't go. Please don't go."

"Sit down, Sis," Uncle Edgar said. "I'll be back."

"Doesn't seem to care for you much, does he?" nagged Sheriff Bonner.

"He does too," I said vehemently. "He's my uncle." This seemed to be enough to prove it.

"I never saw an honest-to-goodness uncle act

like that."

"I like the way he acts," I shouted. And I did. But I wished he would come back.

The slow hours passed and the early winter dark began to come down. Sheriff Bonner had gone to sleep and snored loudly. The horrendous sounds tore at my eardrums; he looked like some terrible animal with his great head doddering around and his mouth open, but anything was better than having him awake.

Every now and then Uncle Edgar stuck his head through the door and looked at me as if to ascertain that I was all right. He didn't come in and I didn't know whether this was because he had been overcome by shyness, after having talked more than I had ever heard him in my life, or simply because he was afraid the sheriff would wake up. I had the impression that he was lurking in the vestibule against any dire emergency that might come up and that made me feel safe and comfortable and sure about everything again . . . sure I wouldn't be tossed in the mailbag and sure my father would be at the station in Porterfield to take me off.

As the afternoon had worn away the weather had changed and it had begun to snow. The sharp wind drove the flakes against the window and the whole world outside was a swirl of white. It had been a rainy winter, full of storms and floods but this was the first snow and I felt gratified that Heaven had come through with the right climate for Christmas. I began to feel drowsy and to think about home and hanging my stocking at the mantel and the Christmas tree and my father and mother and Santa Claus coming down the chimney with the sleepy doll I had ordered. We must be almost to Porterfield by now. We just had to go over the Brazos River Bridge and a little way beyond that was home.

Sheriff Bonner came up out of slumber with a loud snort and roused me from my reverie. He pulled his ponderous watch out and looked at it. "Five o'clock," he said. "Must be about two hours late."

"Two hours late!" I cried. No such exigency had ever occurred to me.

"Yep," he said. "Looks as if you might not get to hang up your stocking after all!"

The full horror of this possibility smote me amidships and I was speechless.

"Well," he said. "I reckon it won't make much difference. You're too old not to know who Santa Claus is."

"Santa Claus is Santa Claus!" I quavered. "I know that."

"Now, Sissy, you can't fool old man Bonner. You're too smart not to know that Santa Claus is just your papa and mamma! A big girl like you."

I was six years old. I was an only child and I had never known many children. The myth was fresh and pure in my mind. Nobody had ever cast a doubt on the authenticity of Santa Claus in my presence. But the horrid truth fell on my ears with the ring of authority. I began to wail.

"He is not! He is not!" I shrieked. The peddler and the sheepherder both started up out of dozes.

"Sure thing. Santa Claus is just your mamma and papa," Sheriff Bonner reiterated loudly.

These words were no sooner out of his mouth than a long, lithe shape leapt like a panther through the doorway leading from the vestibule and Uncle Edgar had Sheriff Bonner by the collar.

"What did you say that for?" Uncle Edgar rasped, shaking the sheriff the way a dog shakes a rat. "Trying to make a little kid miserable. You old devil!"

"Take your hands off me," Sheriff Bonner squeaked trying to reach his gun. "You outlaw!"

Uncle Edgar pinioned his arm, took the gun and threw it into a seat. They began to scuffle up and down the aisle and the men poured out of the smoker into our coach. Uncle Edgar was pummeling the sheriff.

"What's going on?" shouted a drummer.

"He told the little gal there wasn't any Santa Claus," the sheepherder said.

"Why, the old reprobate!" another man yelled. "Let me help you, Edgar."

"I can manage," Uncle Edgar panted, "If I can just keep him in reach."

The peddler put out his foot and tripped Sheriff Bonner as he was backing away and Uncle Edgar landed one glancing blow which caught the sheriff full on the nose. His nose began to bleed and Uncle Edgar let up.

"I reckon that'll hold him," Uncle Edgar said and stood up and hitched up his belt.

"You're under arrest," Sheriff Bonner exploded, holding his handkerchief to his nose which was rapidly beginning to swell.

"Wait'll I tell the judge how this happened," Uncle Edgar sneered.

Sheriff Bonner didn't say anything but departed for the washroom to attend to his swollen nose.

The train suddenly ground to a stop.

Mr. Smith came rushing out of the mail car, staring myopically at the remains of the scene of carnage. "What's going on, boys?" he asked worriedly.

"Just a little private discussion," Uncle Edgar said.

"Ed just decided to whip the sheriff for a Christmas present to himself," one of the other men put in.

"My Lord, this is no time to be fighting," Mr. Smith sighed, his walrus moustache trembling. "It's Christmas Eve. Besides, I've got bad news for you—for all of us." Mr. Smith had a family at the other end of the line waiting to hang up stockings too.

"What is it?" everybody said at once. I had been crouched down in the corner of the seat, my little world a tumbled heap of ruins about me and the sobs strangling my throat, but I sat up and dug my fists into my eyes because Mr. Smith's voice was so sad and worried.

"I just got word—the bridge—" Mr. Smith gulped. "The bridge is blocked over the Brazos. It's a blinding blizzard outside. No chance to get it fixed before tomorrow. Looks like we'll be here all night."

A concerted groan went up and Sheriff Bonner burst out of the washroom to hear the latest disaster. A hubbub of questions, talk, and complaining followed the groan. Not knowing what to do, I began to weep again. They all stopped talking and looked at me and the enormity of the thing broke over them. Here they were, caught for the night in the middle of a prairie in a blinding snowstorm with a girl child whose illusions had just been shattered. And it was Christmas Eve. Distress filled their various faces. They turned to me in despair. Not one of them knew what to say or do.

"Now don't cry, Sissy," Mr. Smith said bravely. "There's not a thing to be afraid of. You'll be home all right tomorrow."

I howled afresh and with increasing volume.

They looked at each other, mutely asking, "What'll we do?"

I continued to bawl.

"You fellows go on up in the smoker," Uncle Edgar said finally with superhuman courage. "I'll try to get her quiet."

They filed out and Uncle Edgar sat down gingerly on the seat beside me.

"I want my mother!" I shrieked, adding, "And there isn't any Santa Claus!" I was unable to separate the two cataclysms in my own mind. One was as bad as the other.

Uncle Edgar fastened on the latter as the more likely topic of discussion. "Now you listen here, Sissy," he said. "There is too a Santa Claus." Uncle Edgar then gathered me in his arms, dying of bashfulness, and proceeded to embroider this theme with what he remembered inexpertly from Clement Moore's Christmas poem on the subject. I think he even recited a few stanzas to prove his point.

He talked and he talked until he was hoarse and at last I began to get sleepy and to believe him.

"But if there is a Santa Claus," I said, "how'll he know where I am—on this old train!" I sniffled again.

"He'll know!" Uncle Edgar put in hastily.

"I want to see him," I insisted, like the arch fiend a six-year-old girl is.

"All right," Uncle Edgar weakly promised. "You'll see him."

Thus reassured, I gave up and sagged against Uncle Edgar's unaccustomed shoulder in the peaceful surrender of sleep.

I don't know how long Uncle Edgar held me there, but it must have been only a few minutes. I have some strange and lingering recollection of his curly hair touching my face and his laying me gently down and covering me with something. I found out later it was his saddle blanket. That was about all he had. All night I had vivid dreams of scurry and bustle and I knew somehow that I wasn't at home and that people were moving about on tiptoe, but I was so worn out by the violences of the day I was never able to get my eyes open.

Nor did I open them until the sunlight, falling through the window of the stalled train and reflecting from the dazzling whiteness of the landscape outside, shone square in my eyes. And what a sight awaited me! They must have put in a night of superhuman endeavor—that ill-assorted group of passengers on the Brazos Valley & Central. They were all standing around in a huddle at one end of the coach, waiting ecstatically for me to become conscious. Young as I was, I saw how pleased they were with themselves and I gave them a brilliant smile.

On the seat opposite me was a pathetic sagebrush scrub which had been uprooted and trimmed with wizened apples, elderly candy and chewing gum, and even a sack of Bull Durham tobacco from the butcher's basket tied on with white twine. On the arm of the seat hung a man's sock, probably from the drummer's suitcase, and this contained one of the most unusual and enticing collections of presents any little girl was ever awarded. There was a rabbit's foot, a string of rattlesnake rattlers which were sometimes worn to cure rheumatism, a deck of cards, slightly used, a large jackknife, a good-luck dollar with a bullet hole through the middle, a small sentimental-looking pair of lady's spurs, and an elk's tooth.

But we still had not reached the climax. When I had examined these tributes with an enthusiasm which I do not have to assure you was not feigned, there was suddenly a great ringing of the train engine's bell and through the mail coach door burst an apparition which had all the ear-marks of Santa Claus. It was fat and shook; it had a mat of silvery whiskers and hair, strangely like sheep's wool. Its eyes were twinkling and it had a large red nose. It had a pack on its back. It capered and cavorted in the approved manner, though somewhat ponderously. The fact that it wore a pair of blue denim overalls and a wind-breaker of the same, and its peaked cap was made of a red bandanna, completely escaped my notice. To my bedazzled eyes, it was certainly Santa Claus, and I thought with renewed wonder, what a miracle it was he had known where to find me, way out here on a dead train in the middle of the prairie.

I do not really know how this oddly-caparisoned figure ever sold itself to my already suspicious mind, but I know it did. I suppose I had the same kind of blind spot most young children have who are able to take all sizes and shapes and costumes of Santa Claus in the stores at Christmas. I desperately wanted to believe that it was true. And so I did.

When the assembled company noted this, a small sigh of relief went up and such jollity broke out as I have never seen before or since. All those sad, homeless men, who would never have been on the Brazos Valley & Central passenger train on Christmas Eve if they had really had any place to go (they were probably all going up to Wichita to get drunk) embraced the Christmas spirit and we were children together. Santa Claus did not open his mouth, but he led a snake dance up the aisle and back and then with a great flourish he put his hand into the pack and from among the shoelaces, saddle soap, needle books, and boxes of arnica, he withdrew a splendid hair ribbon and a china doll without legs, obviously the top of the peddler's one remaining pincushion, and presented them to me. I shrieked with joy, fondled the red ribbon, and folded the maimed baby to my chest.

All my friends were so proud and happy at the success of their hard work. They laughed and slapped each other on the back and the peddler took out a harmonica and played "Dixie" and "When the Work's All Done This Fall." Uncle Edgar did a hat dance, stepping high and delicately around the brim of his Stetson in the intricate steps of the figures. The drummer recited "The Shooting of Dan McGrew" from beginning to end, to loud applause. Mr. Smith, still a little mournful from having missed the hanging of his children's stockings, made me a cat's cradle out of his slightly grimy handkerchief, and the sheep-herder took the jackknife in my loot and carved me a whistle from a small mesquite switch.

While celebration was still at its height, the whistle of the engine gave forth a loud hoot and Mr. Smith ran forward and came back with the news.

"The road's open," he shouted. "We'll be to Porterfield inside of an hour."

I didn't know whether to be glad or sorry, but I didn't have time to think for the Brazos Valley & Central chugged, sighed, picked up steam, heaved, and lurched slowly forward down the snow-laden tracks toward the river. We were going home.

I do not have have to tell you that pandemonium had reigned all night in Porterfield and that my distracted parents could not believe their eyes when I was handed down to them, rosy, smiling, and well pleased with life, my face smeared with the candy I had consumed for breakfast and my arms loaded with strange but compelling presents.

"Santa Claus found me!" I cried, and a sigh went up from the anxious knot of my fellow-passengers, collected in the vestibule to bid me farewell. My Uncle Edgar had a funny grin on his face and his chest seemed to expand.

"Edgar!" my mother cried, noticing him at last. "For heaven's sake—what are you doing there!

Get right off that train and come home to dinner with us."

"Lordy, Ed," my father said, dragging Uncle Edgar off the train just as it was beginning to move toward Wichita. "I'm glad you were on there to look after Sissy."

Uncle Edgar blushed. It was about the first time my father had ever addressed a kind word to him.

"Nothing to it," Uncle Edgar said casually, but he walked straighter. He had at last accepted responsibility, and what's more, he had made good.

Sated with a second Christmas that afternoon, I sat playing with my legless doll among stacks of store-bought presents and my mind began to go over the events of the day. It seemed strange to me that Santa Claus had deigned to visit me in Porterfield and also in the day coach of the Brazos Valley & Central. I told myself that it must have been Santa Claus on the train, because how in the world could somebody who looked so like him have got away out there. And then a sharp thought occurred to me, and I knew once and for all who Santa Claus was. Santa Claus could be anybody, even Sheriff Bonner. The thing that gave it away was not the fact that he was wearing Mr. Bolander's overalls and bandanna or a beard made of sheep's wool right out of that herder's sack or carried the pack that belonged to the peddler, but that he had a bulbous nose—red as a cherry and big only as the nose of Santa Claus, or somebody who has just been hit on it, can be big!

Uncle Edgar had done the whole thing—even to the right kind of nose. I thought of my strange Uncle Edgar with such a surfeit of love that it almost squeezed the wind out of my chest. I immediately transferred all the love I had ever borne Santa Claus to Uncle Edgar, who certainly needed it more. And I swore I would never let him know that I knew.

Years later I did tell him, of course, after he had a little girl of his own. He roared with laughter, remembering it all, especially Mr. Bolander standing in the engine ringing the bell in his long underwear while Sheriff Bonner wore his overalls.

"Naturally he didn't have any yearning to be Santa Claus that day right at first. He was as mad as a hornet already and his nose was swollen and sore. But I persuaded him. A six-gun is persuasive, even to a sheriff, and he'd mislaid his weapon earlier. I reckon that was the last time I ever drew a pistol—last time I had a real right-eous reason to use a gun." Uncle Edgar looked a little sheepish, remembering. "I convinced him that he was the only one for the part—he had the nose for it—and before it was over, he got right into the spirit of the thing.

"Never had any more trouble with old man Bonner from that day on," Uncle Edgar reminisced. "He turned out to be one of my best friends. When I ran for office, he got out and stumped for me. He seemed different to everybody from that time on. Kind of thought of himself as Santa Claus. And the kids used to follow him around. I reckon he was teasing you that day because he really wanted to make up to you. He loved children—never had any family of his own."

I didn't say it, but I thought that Uncle Edgar was always different from that time on too. The angry wildness seemed to go out of him. Shortly after that Christmas, even as my grandmother had hoped, he married a nice girl and settled down. He got so tamed that he rarely ever fell over the furniture and he made a wonderful father. He made a wonderful lawyer too. Maybe you know him, Judge Edgar West of the Court of Civil Appeals?